Mansplainer

A HOT ROMANTIC COMEDY

Mansplainer

A HOT ROMANTIC COMEDY

AVERY FLYNN

Entangled Publishing
644 Shrewsbury Commons Ave
STE 181
Shrewsbury, PA 17361
rights@entangledpublishing.com

Amara is an imprint of Entangled Publishing.

Edited by Liz Pelletier and Lydia Sharp
Cover design by Bree Archer
Cover photography by Art-Of-Photo/Getty Images

Manufactured in the United States of America

First Edition June 2022

At Entangled, we want our readers to be well-informed. If you would like to know if this book contains any elements that might be of concern for you, please check the book's webpage for details.

https://entangledpublishing.com/books/mansplainer

"To be fully seen by somebody, then, and be loved anyhow—
this is a human offering that can border on miraculous."
Elizabeth Gilbert

Chapter One

December 1st...

"I'm getting married. Tomorrow. You're all invited."

If there was anything Nashville "Nash" Beckett could have said to make his entire family go silent for all of ten seconds, that was it. Not that he had planned it to go any differently. When he wanted to make a point, move a plan into action, or motivate an entire room full of the most stubborn and opinionated people in the entire world (aka his family), he knew how to make it happen. That's why he'd known challenging his cousins, Griff and Dixon, to the Last Man Standing bet after their grandma Betty died was always going to end in success.

Manipulative? Him?

Only when he needed to get his family to do what needed to be done for their own good.

The rules of the bet were simple: Each cousin had to go

on six dates with the first woman who answered their dating bios on the Bramble app. The cousin who didn't end up in love by Christmas would officially be named the Last Man Standing and win the most important prize ever: the last Christmas present their beloved grandma Betty left wrapped but untagged.

And he wanted that prize. Bad.

With his other two cousins now deeply in love, he only had to last six dates to be named the winner. Which was why he'd found a loophole, of course. Marriage.

All the Becketts stared bug-eyed at him as they sat around the long table in one of the private dining rooms at Le Hibou, which, despite its name, didn't serve owls (thank fucking God) or French food (again, thank fucking God). It was, however, one of the best (and only) vegan burger joints in Harbor City, which he'd insisted they eat at frequently so his sister, who was the only vegan in the group, didn't always have to be the one scouring the menu for vegan dishes. And honestly, with a restaurant named The Owl, Nash was glad there was no meat being served.

He absently rubbed at his stomach as he glanced around at the decor.

There was a whole owl motif going on, and the chef had named all the burgers after different owls. Now, Nash wouldn't say that the look of the owls fit the look of the people who ordered that type of burger, but he wasn't not saying it, either.

For example, when Nash made his announcement about his wedding, his bearded, tatted-up cousin Griff had been digging into a double-patty Impossible melt called the Whiskered Screech Owl. The man looked like someone you'd cross the street to avoid, and he was prickly enough to be more than happy that people made that assumption, since it usually saved him from having to make small talk. So it was absolutely no shocker Griff was the first Beckett to go back to eating his food at the exact moment when everyone else at the table finished processing Nash's words.

There was a heartbeat more of blessed silence before all the talking started—translation, *hollering*—about a million questions at once. In other words, it was a gathering of Becketts.

Finally, one voice broke through the noise.

"You are so full of shit," his cousin Dixon said and then lifted Fiona's left hand up and kissed it, nearly blinding the room with the light reflecting off the huge diamond engagement ring on her finger.

"Well, actually," Nash said as he squirted ketchup onto his Great Horned Owl, aka a cheeseburger with onion straws. "I'm not. The ceremony is at her apartment. Ten in the morning. The dress code is business casual. There will be a reception afterward. Gifts are not necessary. Now, go back to eating."

Nash knew there was no way they wouldn't show up tomorrow. This bunch was far too curious—fine, too nosy as hell—to skip it.

News delivered and orders given, he went back to eating his burger. Damn, it was fucking delicious.

Everyone at the table continued to gawk at him as he did the smart thing, the logical thing, and continued to eat the best vegan burger in Harbor City while they ignored theirs. They'd regret that. Cold burgers were still good, but nothing like the brain-bending goodness of a warm one. He was about to explain that in detail to them when the giggles started. It began with his sister, Bristol, of course, but pretty soon the whole table was laughing.

Finally catching her breath after her giggle fit, Bristol wiped away a tear of amusement. "Can you imagine?" She used her fork to point at him from her spot at the other end of the table. "This guy? Married?"

Morgan, Griff's little sister, shook her head. "He'd spend so much time explaining how marriages work to his poor fiancée, she'd fall asleep before the proposal."

"Or he'd mansplain how she should feel about engagement rings," Bristol added.

Should he be offended? Maybe, but this was his family, and despite how much he might pretend the opposite was true, he knew their assessment was fair. Not that he'd admit it. He had his reasons, and they knew that. There was a reason why everyone always came to him with their questions and problems—he always knew what to do.

When his mom got stuck in Waterbury because she'd forgotten to pay her cell phone bill—again—he outlined exactly how to set up automatic payments. Information his mom had ignored, per usual. When his brother, Macon, needed help getting his literary agency off the ground? Nash had been there with a business plan within thirty minutes before his brother even got a chance to ask for it. When Bristol had bought that money pit of a house and had no idea where to go for renovation help? He'd outlined her options, developed a pros-and-cons list about contractors, and when she'd ignored him because, as she'd said, she hadn't even asked for his help in the first place, he'd emailed the entire document to her anyway and put in calls to a few of his contacts so she wouldn't get ripped off.

He knew things, and sharing that information was just what he did.

"Is it wrong that I spend enough time reading focus-group reports that I have insight into how people think and how they act?" Nash asked. "I'm literally everyone's best resource. Hell, I'm the family Google."

"Oh my God, Nash. I love you, but you are a dick," Macon blurted out and then looked down to the other end of the table and cringed. "Sorry, Mom."

Okay, so he had a habit of *over*explaining things—even when no one asked for additional information (Bristol and the contractors weren't the only time that had happened). And yes, he had gotten in the habit of anticipating other's moods and reactions, which came in really handy in developing marketing and advertising campaigns at Beckett Cosmetics. He had to know women, the largest percentage of their customer base—although the number of men and nonbinary folks in the makeup and skincare sector was growing—and what would appeal to them. Add to that the fact that he'd grown up as the de facto responsible one who remembered for his parents when the utility bill was due, or to pick up Bristol after her Girl Scouts meeting, or where Macon's baseball team was playing…it was just his wheelhouse.

"You're not even dating anyone," Morgan said. "That's the whole point of this stupid Last Man Standing bet of yours."

"It's not stupid," Nash, Griff, and Dixon said at the same time—and not for the first time. Griff and Dixon were both happily in love and didn't mind not winning the present. Nash, on the other hand, had every intention of being the satisfied recipient of Grandma's gift.

"You can't win by default," Dixon said. "Just being the last man in the running isn't enough."

Nash grinned at his cousin, who hated losing just slightly less than he loved his fiancée. "I wasn't planning on it. The rules we agreed to only state that I have to go out on six dates with a woman who responds to my Bramble dating profile, and I have to make it to Christmas morning without falling in love. There's nothing that says the woman who responds to my ad can't be my wife."

Griff rolled his eyes but took another bite of his double patty melt instead of saying anything—no shocker there.

"So you're what?" Dixon asked, leaning forward and putting his forearms on the table. "Planning on a loveless marriage?"

"The odds are in my favor," Nash said. "Half of all marriages end in divorce."

"Aren't you just a little ray of sunshine," Griff's fiancée, Kinsey, said, her Southern drawl making it sound like it might be a compliment but might also be an insult.

Nash was smart enough to bet on insult.

"Well, actually, I'm just being factual," he said, dragging a french fry through a pool of ketchup before eating it. "Most successful marriages are less about love and more about each person's needs for security and companionship being met. Love doesn't guarantee anything. If you think about how love and lust mess with people's heads, then it probably hurts the chances of a successful marriage."

"Nashville," his mom said, lifting her hand to her chest and setting off a chain reaction of clinking and clacking as her million and one brackets clanged against one another. "Your father and I have been married for forty years, and we're still in love."

And living separately—as in, a five-hour drive from each other—for the past fifteen years, but that worked for them. As far as he could tell, they actually *were* happy with Mom in Harbor City and Dad at a commune upstate.

"Then you're the exception." He glanced over at his engaged cousins. "As I'm sure you'll all be."

"Wow," Dixon said, glaring at Nash. "What a vote of confidence."

"Look, unlike your marriages, my marriage isn't about love." He pushed back from the table and crossed his arms, suddenly losing his appetite even though he had half a burger left. "It's about getting both of us what we want."

"And you want to win the bet," Dixon said.

Nash nodded. "Exactly."

Griff leveled his unwavering stare at Nash. It was a look that could make most people rethink whatever it was they were saying. His cousin's mix of muscles, tattoos, and surly snarl that only left his face when he looked at Kinsey tended to have that effect on people. However, Nash had spent every summer growing up with him and had known him back when he was the runt of the Beckett cousins.

"What's she get?" Griff asked.

Something that wasn't anyone's business. "It doesn't matter. We're both going into this knowing that in a month, on New Year's Eve, our marriage is over. That's more than enough time needed for me to win Grandma Betty's last present and for my wife to accomplish what she needs. One amicable divorce later, and we'll both walk away happily single, unencumbered by love, and with our entire lives ahead of us to do whatever and whoever we want."

His cousins glared at him. They were as close as siblings and as competitive as three nemesis Formula 1 drivers in the race of a lifetime. They'd each walk in front of a crosstown bus for the others but would also gleefully shove a cousin into the icy lake behind Gable House in December just to watch him splutter.

They were guys. It didn't have to make sense.

"This is bullshit," Dixon grumbled, obviously realizing that Nash had outwitted him.

Nash shrugged, relishing the moment. "There's nothing in the rules against it."

"You *wrote* the rules," Griff shot back, no doubt annoyed that the smartest among them hadn't thought of this brilliant idea first.

Nash smirked—he couldn't help it. "No one said life was fair."

"So," Bristol said, yanking Nash's attention back to the

table full of Becketts and soon-to-be Becketts staring him down. "Who is the lucky lady?"

Across the table, his mom gave him an appraising look as she tucked a long hair behind her ear and started off the jingle jangle of her bracelets again. "It's Chelle Finch, I presume."

Nash nodded.

There was a beat of silence, and then everyone—even Griff—asked at the same time, "Who in the hell is Chelle Finch?"

Chapter Two

A few days earlier…

Chelle Finch was T-minus five seconds from losing her shit.

The Finch Foundation had been ignored and all but abandoned by her family when she'd taken it over fifteen years ago. Her father—who had never believed that women, not even his own daughter, should be heading an organization—had figured she couldn't really do any harm to what was essentially a tax write-off. And sometimes when she was alone in the cramped foundation offices late at night, finishing up board reports or reviewing grant proposals, she could still hear his words when he'd given in and agreed to appoint her as the foundation's executive director. She'd gotten the job after months of explaining why she was the best candidate when no one else had accepted the position that paid roughly half of the going rate for the qualifications required.

Her dad had been a quarter through a bowl of plain, watery oatmeal, and he'd let out a woe-is-me sigh before saying, "It'll keep you busy until you finally find a husband."

Yeah, it hadn't been a ringing endorsement by any stretch of the imagination, but she'd seized the opportunity with both hands and had made something of the foundation.

It had gone from being a shell of an organization to actually doing good for people in Harbor City. Not that he'd noticed any of that before he'd had an unexpected fatal heart attack last year. Instead, he'd just called it a distraction from her real job in life—*finding a man to guide her and take care of her.*

She swallowed her anger. There were misogynistic fathers, and then there was her toxic dad, who was king of outdated ideas and just-let-the-menfolk-take-care-of-it bullshit.

Really, was anyone surprised that she spent all of her free time writing fantasy books where the female leads kicked ass?

She'd thought by moving out of the family mansion and remaining single she'd finally escaped the curse hovering over the Finch women that always seemed to land them with some jerk of a man who thought he knew better than any mere woman ever could. So far, it had worked.

But apparently her dad was capable of reaching out from the grave to pull the rug right out from under her sensible shoes today.

Her smarmy jerk of an uncle was more than happy to deliver the news to her as he sat behind Chelle's desk with his size-nine cowboy boots (the ones with the hidden lift insoles) propped up on the battered wood corner. His ten-gallon hat was half on and half off a stack of aid requests sitting in the middle of her desk, making the half-a-foot-high stack look like the Leaning Tower of Pisa. Never mind the fact that in his sixty-five years, the closest Buckley Finch had ever been to a ranch was watching old westerns and rereading every Louis L'Amour book lining the library at his mansion on Eighty-Sixth.

"No one is saying you haven't accomplished, by a miracle no doubt, something that no one thought you possibly could," Uncle Buckley said as he patted down his silver combover, the few strands of which were always popping up anyway despite the amount of hairspray he blasted on it. "But you knew being executive director was a limited-time engagement. The business world is no place for a woman, and your dad cared about you enough to know that you needed a nudge in that direction."

"A nudge?" That's what he was calling this absolute metric ton of bullshit? "Getting slammed by a rocket loaded with billionaires suited up for low atmospheric joyrides in zero G would be less of a nudge than this."

She tucked some of her dark hair behind her ears and took in a deep, cleansing breath, willing herself to calm down. The last thing she needed right now was to appear anything but calm, cool, and collected. Uncle Buckley would seize on the moment to tell her that women were too emotional for leadership positions, she was sure.

He shrugged. "It is what it is, and you knew what was going to happen when your dad's will was read last Christmas."

Chelle's pulse skyrocketed as she fought to keep an even-keel exterior even though, on the inside, she felt like she was drowning. "I never thought my own family would follow his ridiculous dictate."

It really had been too bizarre to even consider. For all of their many faults and toxic attributes, she'd thought her family loved her and finally saw her as a smart, independent, forty-two-year-old woman who had proven herself. That, obviously, had been wishful thinking on her part.

"Your father was right, and you know it." Uncle Buckley

plopped his feet back on the ground and leaned forward, his elbow bumping against his hat, which pushed against the stack of aid requests and sent them tumbling over. He looked at the resulting messy pile in the middle of her desk as if he had no idea how it had happened. "You've played your little game of Boss Lady long enough. You either have a husband by Christmas as required by your father's will, or I become the foundation's executive director and shut the place down." He narrowed his beady little eyes at her. "You could've spent the past year looking for a man who might have let you play executive director on a very part-time basis. Instead, you just stuck your head in the sand and pretended that you could change the way things are."

The urge to rage at this man (the de facto leader of their family and the one who lorded over them all like a real-life Lord Farquaad) rushed up her body like a hot wave of pent-up fury as she sat in the guest chair in her own damn office.

"This isn't the Middle Ages," she said, needing to stay calm because other people's ability to buy groceries, to learn new skills, and to pay daycare bills depended on the foundation continuing its work. "You can't force me to get married or fire me. That's not legal."

"First of all, this is an at-will state. The foundation's board can fire you for any reason or none at all. Secondly, force you to get married?" Buckley's voice went up as if he was shocked—*shocked*—she'd level such an accusation against him. "Michelle Christine Finch, we are only guiding you toward your true calling—being a wife and submitting to your husband. Maybe if your dad had listened to me and put his foot down immediately with you, we wouldn't be in this situation, but here we are."

"This is blackmail." She sank back against the chair, her spine curling into a *C* as her shoulders drooped under the weight of lost hope. "People depend on this foundation. It helps thousands of people every month."

"Yes," Uncle Buckley said, having the audacity to look all torn up about the situation—or as close as he could with a heart as small as a pebble on the beach. "It would be a shame if they suffered because of *your* pride and selfishness."

And there it was, the battle she'd been fighting since she'd come out of the womb without a penis into a family that claimed to believe in traditional values, when it was really all about control. How foolish she'd been to think she'd escaped their clutches and could live as the outcast of one of Harbor City's richest and most powerful families.

"So I get married and that's that? The foundation will be safe?" Chelle asked, fighting for breath as anxiety and a sense of claustrophobia squeezed her lungs.

"Exactly," he said. "It's about time you got with the program. Lucky for you, I have a list of men who would benefit from having you as a helpmate, even if you are much older than a bride should be—especially when it comes to having babies."

Revulsion at the idea of marrying someone her uncle picked, much less having a child with them, rushed through her, and she shot up out of the chair. "No."

He narrowed his eyes at her. "Excuse me?"

"You heard me," she said, shaky from the adrenaline pumping through her veins. She marched the three steps to her office door and yanked it open. "I'll handle the details myself. Now get out."

"You think you can find someone who'd want to marry someone nearly too old to have kids and too fat to be a draw to the marriage bed?" He let out a cruel bark of a laugh. "Good luck with that." He stood up, doing his best, no doubt, to look intimidating. "I'm offering you the only way to keep this foundation going." He plopped his cowboy hat on his head. "You've been to the lawyers—don't think they haven't reached out to me—and you know that there's no way to break your dad's will. It's either you finally take your place as God intended as a wife, or this foundation, which does indeed help the downtrodden here in Harbor City, closes its doors. Of course, I should have known you were too emotional to have a logical, adult conversation." He walked around her desk to the door, pausing long enough to let loose one last barb. "Blessed be, there really is nothing worse than a hysterical woman."

Then he walked out, strutting down the hall like a man who had everything in the world.

Chelle squeezed the doorknob tighter, needing something solid to hold onto. Unless she found a way out of this mess, she was absolutely positive that the foundation's doors wouldn't stay open after the new year.

Chapter Three

It had only been an hour since her uncle had dropped a marriage bombshell and stormed off, but Chelle was still no closer to coming up with a way around this ridiculous demand, and the high-pitched yaps coming from the crate in the corner of her cramped office could not be ignored.

"You two need to go outside?" she asked.

A chorus of doggie squeaks and yips erupted from the crate where her two pugs, Groucho Barks and Mary Puppins, had been tucked in for their fifth of approximately a million naps they took each day.

"Okay, let's do this." She grabbed the leashes from the hook by the door. "You guys are great for helping me plot out my books. Let's see how you do with fighting a real-life evil jerk."

Twenty minutes and two poop bags later, she'd learned the answer to that question was that the dogs were not very helpful at all. She'd spent the whole walk through St. George's

Park going over every option she could think of that didn't involve a wedding and coming up with absolutely nothing. Finally, she sat down at the bench so Mary could sniff every twig and Groucho could roll in the dead leaves with his fat tongue hanging out.

"There has to be a way out of this," she grumbled while the dogs tugged at their leashes as if they had a chance of actually getting the squirrel dashing around just outside of their reach.

But there wasn't—at least nothing she could think of—so she swallowed back the bile burning the back of her throat and started making a list of unmarried men who might be open to marrying a forty-two-year-old with two pugs and an almost feral cat, a second-floor walk-up near the park, four finished fantasy novels under her bed that would never see the light of day, and enough family-related baggage to fill the Grand Canyon.

The list added up to exactly zero point zero.

She dropped her chin to her chest in defeat. "I am so screwed."

"Oh, darling," a woman said, then made a sympathetic clucking sound.

Chelle looked up at the woman who'd stopped in front of the park bench. Dressed in a voluminous pure-white faux-fur winter coat that was left open despite the cold wind rattling the trees' bare limbs, the woman smiled. Her purple lipstick matched her brightly colored floral muumuu and the colored tips of her wild gray curls that were escaping from the messy bun on top of her head.

"That does not sound like it's the good kind of screwed at all," the woman said.

Shocked into responding, Chelle nodded. "Not even close." Then without meaning to, she tacked on, "I've got less than a month to come up with a way to defy my dad's will or find someone to marry me for a charity."

"Oh my." The woman's face softened with sympathy as she shook her head and said, "No one would think it a charity to marry you. You must think more of yourself, darling."

Embarrassed heat flooding her cheeks, Chelle opened her mouth to explain the woman had misheard her, she literally had to marry *for a charity*, but the woman sat down next to Chelle on the bench.

"What you need," she said with an excited gleam in her eye, "is a reading."

Then she whipped out a deck of tarot cards from her large purse and started shuffling. After a few fast rounds of mixing the cards, the woman set the deck down between them and tapped it. "Hold your hands on the deck and think of your question."

Sucked in by the woman's off-kilter but just-here-to-help vibe, Chelle did as she was told. She closed her eyes and pictured Uncle Buckley's little rat face and concentrated on the question of how to save the foundation without damning herself to a life of wifely submission.

"Excellent," the other woman said when Chelle opened her eyes again. "Cut the cards and let's get started."

With the strict and sheltered way she'd grown up, Chelle had limited experience with tarot readings, but this reading was unlike any other Chelle had seen in movies or in the banished books she'd devoured the minute she'd moved out of her parents' house.

The charitable would have called the woman's tarot technique unconventional.

The purists would have called it a horror show.

The woman's gold bracelets, with a dozen charms hooked to each one, jingled and jangled as she laid out the cards. Instead of a simple three- or five-card spread, she made a circle out of seven cards but only read three she seemed to pick at random.

"Oh, fantastic," the woman said as she turned over a card with the word DEATH scrawled across the bottom of it in hot pink ink. "It's a time for new beginnings and"—she flipped over one labeled THE KNIGHT OF WANDS— "adventure and"—she revealed a card with ACE OF CUPS in block letters at the top—"relationship help is on the way."

"In the form of a tall, dark stranger?" Chelle asked, as jumpy as if a whole hive of wasps was under the bench at the sight of the death card. New beginnings yes, but death all the same.

"No." The woman swept up the cards and piled them onto the rest of the deck. "He's blond, but my son Nash is perfect for this job. He always has the answers, or at least thinks he does. He'll know just what to do."

Okay, this encounter had definitely gone from quirky to possibly serial killer-y. Chelle briefly wondered what the woman's son would think of his mother volunteering him to help a stranger. "That's sweet, but I'm not sure that—"

"Oh, not to worry. Nash will be sure enough for forty people." The woman held out her hand. "I'm Celeste Beckett. I'm so glad the universe put me in your path today. We're going to get along famously."

"Chelle Finch." She shook Celeste's hand. "Nice to meet you, but I'm not sure your son can help."

If none of the lawyers could, what was he going to be able to do?

"Of course he can, dear. He just always does," she said. "He can fix anything."

And what did it say that talking to the dog park's surprise tarot reader's son was the best option Chelle had? Bad things, it said very bad things.

But what other choice did she have? Too many people depended on the foundation for Chelle to just give up without a fight. And if that meant talking to random strangers with super problem-solving powers...so be it.

This was nuts. And she was doing it anyway.

"As long as we can meet in public"—Chelle said, wondering what in the world she was doing—"then I'm in."

Chapter Four

It was noon on a Tuesday, and Nash was at St. George's Park on a mission for his mom instead of meeting with a cosmetics buyer with the biggest luxury retail store in Australia. The buyer was interested in stocking Beckett Cosmetics' products, a deal that would improve the company's bottom line by 15 percent. That wasn't just a lot of zeroes, it was the kind of growth that could take Beckett Cosmetics to the next level in the international market.

It was a fucking *massive* deal.

That's why he should have told his mom "no" when she'd called last night, instead of rearranging his entire schedule to accommodate this "teeny tiny little favor," as she'd put it.

But he hadn't.

Now, here he was freezing his balls off as the first snow of the season fell, looking for a woman his mom had said needed his help.

Fuck. He was such a sucker.

Grumbling to himself, Nash rounded a bend in the treelined asphalt path and stopped a few steps beyond the reach of an eighty-pound lab testing its leash and its owner's strength while doing its best to get to a squirrel that was staring down at it from a just-high-enough branch. The dog's owner, meanwhile, was searching one-handed through the pockets of her thick wool coat while standing next to a giant, steaming mound of poop that only a dog of the lab's size could produce.

"Damn it," she grumbled.

After switching his to-go cup of coffee to his right hand, Nash reached into one of the inside pockets of his coat and pulled out one of the plastic poop bags he'd stuffed in there, because his mom would forget hers every time she went on a walk with her demon Jack Russell-chihuahua mix. "Need one of these?"

"Oh my God, yes," the woman said with a relieved smile. "Thank you!"

"No worries." He handed the bag over. "You know, they make these poop bag holders that clip right onto the leash so you don't have to worry about forgetting them when you leave the house for a walk. Or you could leave some right next to the leash as a visual cue. Or you could—"

The woman lifted her hand in the air, the one holding the now-full poop bag, and glared at him. "I think I got it."

That look. He knew that look. Narrowed eyes. Set jaw. I-have-had-enough tension in the other person's shoulders.

Okay, she was pissed.

"Of course you do," he said, trying to explain it so that she saw he wasn't meaning to be an asshole. "It's just that there are tricks you can use—"

"I've had dogs my entire life," she nearly growled out, causing her dog to forget about the squirrel and move closer to her, doing a lab's best version of a doggie glare, which—to be honest—wasn't very intimidating. "Trust me, I got it."

Way to go, Beckett. You couldn't just keep your big-ass mouth shut like everyone tells you?

"Yeah, okay," he said, already moving away. "Sorry."

Nash took a swig of the lukewarm coffee and continued down the path, crunching on the last of the season's red-and-yellow leaves scattered across the asphalt getting dusted with snow.

Why had he agreed to meet this woman in a *dog park*, of all places?

It wasn't like he had a dog. There was no room in his life for that. He was too busy making sure his amicably-living-apart parents didn't drown in overdraft fees, since his father, who had given up all of the money and business connections to Beckett Cosmetics before retiring to a commune upstate, and his mom relied on "the universe" to take care of all of life's mundane tasks. They weren't bad people. They just didn't do well with the daily business of life.

Then there were his younger brother and sister, who he insulated from having to deal with any of their parents' laissez faire disasters as much as possible. Bristol and Macon had their own lives that didn't need to be centered around making sure their mom didn't live in the dark and their dad didn't go to jail for bouncing too many checks.

Nash was the oldest.

Keeping everyone on top of things and out of trouble was his job.

And that's why he was here, in a dog park, searching for his mom's friend—because she needed help, and that's what he did.

The fenced dog run was up ahead, along with an open-air café that offered human *and* dog snacks. His mom had told him that Chelle Finch would be waiting for him there and that he'd know her when he saw her. When he'd pressed for more details—even hair color—his mom had said the universe would let him know and promptly hung up the phone.

Scanning the people sitting outside the café, he spotted a couple with matching mustaches take turns feeding a Pomeranian with a pink bow, a woman in enough outerwear she looked more at home on the tundra than Harbor City on a thirty-degree day like today, and a waitress in a cat-ear headband, telling a Doberman that looked like it might eat a small child that he was the most handsomest good boy in the whole dog park.

There wasn't any lightning strike of recognition, no smack to the back of the head from the universe, and definitely no ah-ha moment. Instead, there were only a blustery late-November day and a handful of people and their dogs.

"Oh my God!" a woman screeched from behind him. "Sir Hiss! Stop!"

Nash felt the piercing jabs on his back a half second before their meaning sank in half as deep as the cat's claws had. Then it was just straight-up shock as the cat climbed up Nash's back, using its claws as spikes to pierce his coat and sink down to his skin. It didn't stop until the feral animal was perched on top of his head like some kind of demon cat mountain climber. Nash didn't move. He couldn't. He could barely breathe without the cat sinking its claws deeper into his scalp. The excited, high-pitched yaps of two small dogs and the woman still calling out after "Sir Hiss" got closer. He would have turned, but any sudden movement seemed like the worst of all possible ideas.

On the inhale, he started to slowly raise his free hand to get ahold of the feline hissing from its unauthorized spot.

That's exactly when disaster struck.

Suddenly, two black pugs were running circles around his shins, their leashes tightening with each turn, while the cat angrily yowled from the top of his head. The leashes forced his legs closer together like a wobbly tree trunk as the dogs bounced off of him, making it hard to stay upright. In an effort to keep his balance, he threw out his arms, being careful not to scare the cat into digging deeper with its claws or sending coffee spilling out of his cup and onto the dogs.

From the top of his head, the cat let out a series of angry hisses, slashing at the air with one paw, claws extended.

"Sir Hiss. No!" The woman on the other end of the dogs' extended leashes rushed closer with every doggie rotation, her full, round cheeks pink from the chilly breeze. She yelled out, "I'm so sorry, I—Groucho Barks! Mary Puppins! Leave it!"

The pugs, their eyes bulgy from excitement and tongues fat from exertion, promptly sat down in front of him, loosening his bonds enough that he could step out. Holding his breath, he lifted one leg. The cat spooked. Body vibrating with fury, it yowled and launched itself off Nash's head. Its back paws delivered a nasty swipe as it used Nash's skull as a springboard to fly through the air and land on the woman's shoulder, like a demented parrot instead of the freaked-out cat that it was.

Forehead hurting like a son of a bitch, Nash let out a grunt of pain. In response to the noise, the dogs still at his ankles started yapping and running around him again, their leashes catching on his right foot. The next thing he knew, he was falling backward. He tossed his coffee cup in the opposite direction from the woman and her personal zoo as he threw his arms outward in a desperate attempt to regain his balance.

It didn't work.

On the inhale he had the path under his feet, and on the exhale his ankle made a weird popping sound. He had half a second to register the oh-shit moment before he was ass-down in a snowy puddle.

His ass hurt.

His ankle hurt.

His fucking pride hurt.

"Oh my God!" the woman said, squatting down and leaning over him. "I am so sorry. Are you okay?"

"I'm fine," he all but growled, sounding more like his always-surly cousin Griff than himself.

"Here, let me help you." She reached out right as the cat snarled and the dogs started barking at him as if *he* had knocked *her* on her ass.

He planted his palms on the asphalt and started to stand up. "I got it."

That's when he finally gave the woman a good look. Tall and extra curvy, with dark, nearly black, thick hair laced with a few gray strands, she was bundled up in a coat, hat, and scarf, like someone about to go on an arctic adventure instead of leisurely walking their animals in the park. She had deep laugh lines framing her eyes and lips that were plump enough to give a man ideas. To put it bluntly, she could be in a modern take on a Rubens painting—curvaceous, sexy, and definitely up to something.

Yeah, that's exactly what you should be thinking about while you're on your ass in a puddle in the middle of helping your mom's friend. Dumb ass.

He pressed against the cement and pushed himself upright, keeping an eye on the pugs that kept their attention focused on the cat, who was ignoring all of them as if he hadn't started the entire thing.

The small orange tabby wore some kind of vest-slash-harness thing attached to a leash and had tucked up close against the woman's bright green coat.

Good God, she was the kind of person who walked her cat.

"You know, unless the cat is trained and likes it, walks

can be really stressful for them." He reached back in his memory for the internship he'd done in college with a focus group company that specialized in pet supplies. "They often will act out and can become aggressive. Negligent pet owners who ignore that very understandable response risk their cat getting hurt or labeled a problem pet by animal control. I'd highly recommend you talk with—"

He put his full weight down on both feet, and the sudden blast of pain in his ankle killed the words on his tongue.

"Oh crap, you're hurt." The woman rushed to his side, managing to put the cat on the ground and switch all three leashes to her left hand before scooting under his arm and wrapping her right arm around his waist. "I live right across the street. You can put that up and decide if you want to call an ambulance or an Uber or something."

There was no way going with this woman was a good idea—and yet, when she started leading him toward the park's exit, he was hobbling along beside her.

"I'm Chelle Finch," she said, looking both ways before they jaywalked across Jackson Avenue and made it through traffic.

Shocked, he nearly tripped over absolutely nothing as they stepped up onto the sidewalk from the street. "Seriously? I'm Nash Beckett."

She whipped her head around to look up at him, her brown eyes round as a pair of Oreos. "Oh shit."

"Exactly."

Well, his mom would be thrilled he found her, but he really would have preferred if the universe had taken a less painful route to making introductions. At least it couldn't get any worse.

As they approached Chelle's building, he reached up and brushed away the sweat beading on his forehead and starting to drip into his eyebrows. But it wasn't sweat. His fingertips were red with blood. His mouth went dry at the same moment his hands got clammy.

Oh God, not that—anything but blood.

It wasn't a lot, but it was enough. His gut clenched as the busy Harbor City sidewalk turned hazy and the world wobbled before his eyes.

"Nash," Chelle called out.

He half turned toward her, moving in slow motion. Then the ground traded places with the sky, and he was on his ass in a puddle of melted snow for the second time in fifteen minutes.

Chapter Five

Her thick thighs were saving lives. Literally.

Okay, maybe not literally, but it was Chelle's strong legs that were helping to get a wobbly kneed, but thankfully not as ghostly white, passed out anymore, know-it-all down the second-floor hall to her apartment.

Her dogs barked their encouragement from a few steps ahead while her cat watched the entire process from the welcome mat in front of the door, with a look of total contempt. If it had been anyone else, she would be laughing—how could a person not in this ridiculous situation? Here she was, with her arm around a guy who was a solid foot taller than her and wider than her size-sixteen self, slow-walking down her hallway because her cat had tried to slice and dice him while her dogs had gone for a little light bondage in public.

Did her brain go to bondage while holding onto a guy so solid he seemed like he'd tell a tree how to tree? Yeah.

What could she say, she was a woman who wrote erotic fantasy stories based very loosely on Greek myths with bisexual double-dicked satyrs and nymph assassins working together to save the world, so "going there" was kind of in her wheelhouse. Never mind the fact that she never actually submitted her stories to a publisher and that all of them had ended up printed out, bound, and in a box in her front closet. She was a woman with a vivid imagination, and she liked using it.

Plus, she was a sucker for whatever cologne Nash was wearing. It was just woodsy and manly enough that she was having way too many mental images of a guy who looked a lot like him with the perfect level of Viking-rugged-lumberjack bod sitting half naked in front of a fireplace and reading *The Fifth Season* by N.K. Jemisin out loud to her. Yes, he'd totally do *all* the voices.

That fantasy was enough to block out the shakes in her thighs—from overwork and not because she kept taking extra sniffs of him, even though she had (a fact she'd spend the rest of her life not telling anyone) as they got closer to her apartment.

"It's the next door on the left," she said.

"The yellow one?" He shook his head and made the same disappointed clucking sound his mom had made at the park yesterday. "You should consider matching your neighbors' doors. The yellow makes it stand out and could make you an easier target for someone unsavory."

She laughed, a harsh blast of sound that sounded about as joyful as burned popcorn tasted. "I'm a round woman in her forties who is forever single. I stand out no matter what." She fished her keys out of her pocket on her non-Nash side and unlocked her door. "Besides, I like this goldenrod shade of yellow."

That seemed to shut him up, but only until they got

inside. He stood in the middle of her living room, weight all on his right foot, as she cleared the stack of books on the closest chair so he could sit down, and took a look around her pre-war apartment.

She'd inherited the place from her great-aunt Katherine, the only other female Finch to rebel against the confining familial bonds of being a Finch. Her great-aunt had started the process of taking the neutral color palette beloved by their taupe-is-color-enough family and injecting the hand-finished plaster walls with bright, glorious color—and Chelle had continued the tradition.

She'd spent the fall sanding down the built-in bookcases in the living room and then staining them a peacock blue that looked gorgeous with the sun coming in from the oversized leaded-glass window that overlooked the park. Next on her list was to strip all of the white paint from the fireplace surround and bring it back to its original red brick. There were a pair of matching leopard-print dog beds on either side of the hearth, a custom-built catwalk for Sir Hiss that went across the top third of the window, and parquet-patterned hardwood floors that had enough coats of industrial-strength polyurethane to protect it when Groucho Barks and Mary Puppins got the zoomies.

"Is that a sword?" Nash asked, looking at the Claymores hanging above her fireplace that had been the inspiration for the hero's weapon of choice in her second book.

"Yes." She unhooked the dogs' leashes from their collars, and they took off running to the water bowl in the kitchen. "Here, you sit down, and I'll get a bandage for your head. Then we can take a look at your ankle."

After he settled into the chair and put his foot up on the deep merlot–colored storage ottoman also filled with books, she hurried into the kitchen. She grabbed the bandages and hydrogen peroxide from the cupboard by the fridge, filled a plastic baggie with ice, and then snagged a clean washcloth from under the bathroom sink and got it wet enough to clean up the one-inch slice Sir Hiss had made to the guy's forehead.

Arms full of Florence Nightingale supplies, Chelle walked through the arched opening from the hall back into the living room and came to a dead stop.

Nash sat there in the chair, with Sir Hiss making biscuits on his thigh.

Seeing her cat do that was weird enough to make her pause, considering his fuck-you attitude toward almost everyone.

But what really had her frozen to the spot was the fact that Nash had taken off his camel-colored topcoat and was sitting there in a cream sweater with its sleeves pulled up to almost his elbows and a pair of navy trousers, the inseam of which were doing the Lord's work to keep it together around his solid-oak thighs. Blond hair, with dimples that never quite went away even when he wasn't smiling, and a square jaw, Nash Beckett was very much *not* her type. There wasn't a tattoo, a piercing, or even a smidge of the kind of trouble that acted like honey for nearly any woman who'd broken free from a claustrophobically set-in-the-fifties patriarchal family.

And yet…

Damn, she really needed to re-download the dating apps she had deleted for the fiftieth time. Her fingers and her vibrator were good, but sometimes the only thing that took the edge off was the *D*.

And did her gaze drop down to his lap?

Yes, it did.

Fuck. She really needed to pull it together.

"You know," Nash said, ruining the delightfully dirty direction of her thoughts by opening his mouth and letting rip with the one-way conversation starter preferred by mansplainers everywhere, "if that sword fell from the wall, it could damage the wood floor or even hurt your pets."

God, why did hot men have to ruin everything by talking? "Good thing I have it well secured, then."

"Are you sure?" He started to get up, annoying the cat, who jumped off his lap and stalked off. "I can double check it."

"They're fine," she said as she crossed over to where he was before he could put any weight on his sore ankle. "Now sit back down."

He looked like he was going to argue for a second but to her relief settled back down into the chair and put his foot on the ottoman again. After making sure the plastic baggie was closed all the way, she pushed the leg of his pants up, rolled down his tan-and-brown argyle sock, and checked his ankle. She wasn't a doctor, but she'd played in enough field hockey games growing up to know what to do with a banged-up ankle. Nash's was swollen but not ballooning up. That was a good sign.

"Are your toes tingling or numb?" she asked.

He shook his head as he wiggled his toes and then rolled his ankle, only grimacing a little.

"Good. It looks like it's only a mild sprain." She let out a relieved breath—not just because she didn't want to see anyone get hurt but because she also didn't want to get sued, something she knew from her own family that rich people loved to do, and there was no way with that fine of a bespoke topcoat that Nash Beckett didn't have money. And unlike the rest of her family, her bank account was nowhere near healthy enough for her to get sued by someone with too much money and time on their hands. "You just need some ice, rest, and elevation, but if the pain gets worse, you'll need to go see a doctor."

"Yes, ma'am."

She rolled her eyes at him, but he just grinned back at

her, the dimples in both cheeks giving him a charming vibe instead of a smarmy one. Now that was a good trick. She made a mental note to give her satyr hero a dimple—only one, though, because two was a little overwhelming.

"Now to that cut," she said as she picked up the damp washcloth.

Standing close and leaning over him a bit, she dabbed at the laceration, glad to see it wasn't bleeding much anymore, which was amazing because she was late on trimming Sir Hiss's nails and those babies were little knives right now.

"That's a lot of books," he said, referring to her stuffed bookshelves.

"All the better to read away the long, cold nights."

Fine. Maybe three floor-to-ceiling bookshelves was a bit much, but she was a woman with an indie bookstore within walking distance and they welcomed well-behaved pets— which meant they made an exception for hers.

"You know," Nash started in with that icepick of a know-it-all tone, "if you rearranged the books into alphabetical order, it would be easier to manage your collection."

"Actually, I like them organized by color." The bright rainbow of printed friends made her smile whenever she walked into the living room.

"But if you alphabetized them, it would be so much easier to find what book you're looking for." He winced a bit when she dabbed hydrogen peroxide on his cut. "And what about moving the couch so it's not in front of the window but nearer the fireplace?"

Oh my God. Did the man not stop? She at least was starting to see why his mother felt so confident her son would know exactly how to help her fix her problem with her father's will. Was there anything this guy didn't think he knew the answer for?

"The dogs spend most of the day watching the

neighborhood goings on from the back of the couch," she said between clenched teeth as she used the washcloth again to clean up the hydrogen peroxide where it had run a bit down his forehead.

"Are you sure that's a good idea?" he asked, obviously not taking the hint. "I know they're small, but their weight is enough to pull the seams of the cushions. That would be a real headache to fix and—"

Chelle held up the damp washcloth, putting the corner that had turned a very light pink from the cut on his forehead right in front of his eyes.

All of the color drained from his face, and he gulped. "That's not fair."

"No." She folded up the cloth so he couldn't see the stained side. "But it got you to stop mansplaining my own apartment decor to me."

He opened up his mouth as if he was going to make another run at the topic, closed it for a second, and then said, "Mom said you need help."

"I do, but I don't think you'll be able to do anything," Chelle said as she put a bandage over his cut with hands that shook just enough to remind her to take a deep breath before all the anger at the injustice of it all swirling around in her belly took over. "I have to break a condition of my father's will, and every lawyer I've talked to said it can't be done." She stood up and gathered the cloth, the brown bottle of hydrogen peroxide, and the bandage wrapper. "If I can't, then control of the charity foundation I've dedicated my life to running goes to my uncle, who would love nothing more than to shut it down or turn it into a paper charity. I mean, the foundation has a board, but they'll fall in step behind my uncle. He has all the right connections to press his point. I can't let that happen."

Her heart was going a million miles an hour, and if she

clamped her teeth together any tighter she was going to crack a molar, but she held onto her control. Giving in to the fury never helped when it came to her family.

"What's the will require?"

"That I get married," she said.

Did it come out like she'd said bury herself in a hole so deep she'd disappear completely? Well, that tracked, because that's the type of marriage her father had no doubt envisioned for her.

"There is no way that's legal," Nash said.

"Well, according to the lawyers I've talked with, the wording in my father's will skirts that line just enough to make it work." Dread and a sense of powerlessness ate away at her stomach lining. "And after they fire me as the Finch Foundation's executive director, Uncle Buckley will install some figurehead to keep the foundation functioning enough to be a tax write-off, but that'll be it. It'll be a shadow of its former self."

The dogs scurried closer, rubbing their hard little heads against her calves in an obvious effort to comfort her, but Chelle couldn't stop. The words just poured out, frustration thick with each syllable coming out of her mouth. "I've talked to the lawyers, they're willing to go to court, but at most, it'll just be a delay of the inevitable. Either I get married and get a judge to agree it's a valid marriage or Uncle Buckley gets control of the foundation."

By the time she finished, her lungs tight with fury at how unfair and just plain wrong it all was, the pugs were wiggling and prancing in place at her feet, yapping and howling in solidarity—obviously not knowing who they were mad at, but if Chelle was mad, so were they. And people wondered why having pets was so amazing. They didn't worry about what other people thought or needed to adhere to some outdated ideas about gender roles. They loved, they were loyal, and when it looked like the shit was about to hit the fan, they were there. If only she could find human beings who were like that—who didn't only live between the covers of a book.

"I'm sorry, babies, Mommy just got fired up about Uncle Fuckley," Chelle said in a soothing tone as she pat the now-quiet pugs on their heads before looking over at Nash, nailing him to his chair with a glare. "And no, I don't need you to explain to me about training my dogs to calm down. I do not need a man to tell me my own business. Not today. Not tomorrow. Never again."

If he understood that her last statement was to put him in his place, Nash Beckett didn't show it. Instead, he looked up at her with a confidence bordering on cocky.

"But I know exactly what needs to happen," he said, sitting forward in his chair, a huge smile on his face. "We have to get married."

That was the most asinine thing she'd ever heard. Chelle stared at him for a moment in shock before the absolute, undeniable ridiculousness of the idea hit her and all she could do was laugh. It wasn't a little giggle or a hearty chuckle. It was a big, throw-your-head-back, evaporate-all-of-your-worries-for-a-moment belly laugh that left her breathless with a goofy grin on her face by the time she finally stopped.

"Oh my God. I needed that," she said, wiping tears from her eyes. "Getting married to anyone—let alone getting married to a total stranger—is what I'm trying to avoid."

"Marriage will fix it all," he said, looking as if he was already putting together a mental plan to share the news with their families. "We only have to stay together long enough to get a judge to declare you married and, therefore, having met the terms of your father's will—which doesn't mention anything about a quick divorce afterward, I'm hoping."

He grinned bigger when Chelle shook her head no. "Perfect. And for me to win a little bet I've got going with my cousins, I just have to date a woman and *not* fall in love. There's nothing in the rules saying I can't date my wife." He clapped his large hands together and looked up at her. "We can start the divorce proceedings on New Year's Eve, both of us with everything we wanted. There is no downside to this."

Nash Beckett was a puppy of a man, the kind who'd always had everything go his way.

Okay, fine. He didn't look like a puppy.

When he was standing upright, he towered over Chelle's five feet six inches. He had a jaw that was square enough to make Superman weep with jealousy. Then there was the fact that he had sandy blond hair that waved just enough to make a woman who hadn't settled into permanent singledom want to run her fingers through it. Add to that, he had these ice-blue eyes that Chelle could easily imagine staring into over gin and tonics at night and mugs of hot tea the next morning. All of it added up to Nash Beckett being not a puppy but a very big dog—perfect for a young, cute, thirty-something woman with a high tolerance for mansplaining and the patience for rearranging her life to make room for another person.

Chelle was not that woman.

Not even close.

She was a no-fucks-left-to-give forty-two-year-old who was not going to adjust her life to fit with another person. She had her pets, her books she wrote and never shared with another soul, and her determination to somehow—anyhow— keep Uncle Buckley's boney little fingers off of the trigger of the gun he aimed at the foundation. It was almost enough to fill all of her time.

Fine.

She could use another project or five beyond all of that and learning to stilt-walk to fill up the hours, but that didn't mean she wanted a man. She had batteries, a vivid imagination, and the internet in all of its porny glory. The last thing she wanted was a husband—especially one who liked to tell her *her* own business.

Ha!

Not in this lifetime, and probably not in the one after it, either.

Still, her interest was piqued, and she hadn't been able to think of another solution since her dad's will was read almost a year ago. That was never a good combination. Plus, her writer brain really wanted to know about what was in it for him.

"What's your bet with your cousins?"

He let out a resigned sigh. "It's to go out on six dates with the same woman who responds to the Bramble bio by Christmas and not fall in love with her."

Too bad for the young pup sitting across from her, the years when that would have made her stop everything to pitch in and help were gone. She was a grown-ass woman. She didn't play anymore.

"Yeah, no. I'm gonna have to turn down your unusual proposal. I'll figure out another way. I have to." She let out a weary sigh, because she really was too old for the kind of bullshittery that went with having a man in her life. "Sorry again for Sir Hiss and the dogs. Do you need me to call someone to give you a ride home?"

Chelle was turning toward the kitchen to put away her nursing supplies when Nash reached out, his hand stopping millimeters from hers and setting off every one of her oh-hey-there-we-liked-that-a-lot nerves that went straight to her clit.

Whatever.

So it had been all batteries all the time for too long. That didn't mean she needed to change anything about how she was living her life. She was more than fine.

He pulled his hand back without actually touching her, flexing his fingers as he did so. "It really could work."

She was about to tell him to forget it—again—when that little nugget of a question popped in her head. It was a "what if" that usually meant the perfect idea for a book, but this time it was all about real life and having an opportunity that very few women who've had to deal with a mansplainer ever get. A giddy thrill zoomed through her and had her clasping her hands together so she didn't clap with excitement.

"Only if I can give you a mansplainer makeover," she said, turning the very bad—and yet very, very good—idea around in her head.

It was the kind of idea that probably wouldn't work out, but if it did...*oh! If it did*. It was as enticing as that late-night declaration from a friend that one more shot of tequila wouldn't do any harm. So salut and cheers to the universe, because she was going to go for it even if this idea would leave her with a massive hangover and all the regrets.

"Agreed." He nodded. "Just tell me what to do."

One of her eyebrows shot upward, almost of its own free will, because there was no way he wasn't full of shit. "That was a quick yes."

He grinned, showing off just how big both of his dimples were, and any hope she had of resisting this delicious idea began to disintegrate.

Tempting? Oh my God was this tempting.

"And you'll do whatever I say?" That seemed like fun. How many times had she wanted to set a man who thought he knew everything right back into his own lane? And now she could actually do it? And he was asking for it?

"Actually, that's not exactly how a makeover works. You see—" He shut his mouth and pursed his lips together. "Fuck. Sorry."

Her laugh exploded out of her, loud and full of amused joy.

Well, she had been thinking about starting another

project. This could be Operation Nash Doolittle. Really, she'd be doing the women of Harbor City a favor.

Still, she couldn't shake the last little crumbs of hesitation.

"I'm nearly ten years older than you are, at a guess. I could have been your babysitter," she said, even as she began to mentally crush those crumbs. "No one would believe we would get married for real. Uncle Buckley would see it for the farce it is and convince the judge we're trying to defraud the court."

"Trust me, I sell people on ideas for a living. They'll believe us," Nash said, his gaze dipping down to her mouth before snapping back up. "It would only be for a month—long enough for me to win the bet and for you to satisfy the rules of the will. All you have to do is respond to my Bramble dating bio and then we get married. It's easy and will fix everything. You know it will. Anyway, do you have a better plan?"

The answer to that was a firm no.

The whole idea of getting married was awful. There was a reason why married men lived longer on average than married women. Marriage was work—a lot of it done mostly by the wife—made bearable because the people involved loved each other. Chelle didn't even know Nash Beckett, let alone love him.

But she also didn't know of another way to keep her uncle from defunding the charitable foundation if he got his hands on it. Marrying Nash would satisfy the requirement of her dad's will.

It was her only option. She had to bite the veil and get married.

Chapter Six

Nash

Because the key to his plan was shock and awe, he wasn't going to tell his family about the wedding until tonight's dinner at Le Hibou. That would get all of the Becketts talking to each other about him rather than focusing on him and why he should change his mind. He knew his people. They needed to be properly managed.

That's why he'd ditched today's usual takeout in the boardroom at Beckett Cosmetics with his cousins before their weekly company meeting. He'd told Dixon, the company CEO, and Griff, the former head of R&D, that he had to take a client out to lunch.

In reality, he was pacing the marble hall in front of the county clerk's office at the Harbor City Town Hall and checking the time on his phone every third step, grinding his teeth as he wondered if she'd really show for the appointment to get their wedding license.

He'd texted directions to Chelle, including a link to the

courthouse on Google Maps. He'd offered to send an Uber to pick her up, but she'd turned him down. He'd said he'd meet her at her place and they could go together. She'd told him he was being annoying and to stop it.

He'd kept texting but had deleted each message after that.

Maybe he shouldn't have.

Maybe he should have insisted on offering his help.

Fuck.

Grinding his teeth, he checked his phone for the millionth time as he headed for the front doors. He could be at her place in twenty minutes. He grasped the oversize brass handle and swung the door open. A gust of cold air blew in, along with the sound of an excited low bark. Chelle was halfway up the wide steps, headed in the direction of a bored-looking police K-9 standing with its handler at the base of the stairs.

Was he a total asshole for taking a moment to appreciate the view?

Yes. He was.

He looked anyway.

Chelle didn't look like the frigid wind blasting down Fourth Avenue could send her flying. Her smile was wide and full. Her ass was high and round, the kind that a man would need both hands to hold onto—not that he would be doing that no matter how abso-fucking-lutely she checked off every one of his boxes on his thank-God-for-thick-women checklist.

This was a mutually beneficial marriage of convenience for a limited duration. Sex would only complicate things. He hated complications. He had enough to keep track of as it was when it came to running Beckett Cosmetics and his family's lives.

Still, he took a second look.

Then a third.

And he was a good ten seconds into the fourth when her

husky voice cut through the fantasies he was starting to run through his head.

"Oh, you're not that scary at all, are you, you sweet little furball? Now give me your paw and you'll get the treat," Chelle said, her voice firm as she planted a hand on one of her generously round hips and held aloft in the other a Milk-Bone dangling from the tips of her fingers as she stared down at the police dog. "Paw, Georgette."

The woman's dog obsession was a menace. She was going to get eaten or arrested or arrested and then eaten. He couldn't let that happen.

Nash hurried down the steps, getting to Chelle's side prepped and ready to dive between her and the jaws of death just when the German Shepherd lifted its right paw.

"Oh, what a good girl you are," Chelle praised the K-9 as she gave it a treat. "Darnell, your mom was right. Georgette really is the sweetest girl."

Some of the confused shock Nash was trying to process must have shown on his face, because when Chelle looked up, she took pity on him. She chuckled, the sound full-bodied, like an aged whiskey with a complex flavor profile that knocked a guy back on his heels and said, *You've never had anything like me before and you never will again.*

"Darnell, meet my soon-to-be husband, Nash. And Nash"—she tucked a long section of salt-and-pepper hair behind her ear as the wind tugged at the rest of it—"meet Darnell, my best friend Karmel's recently married son and his K-9 partner, the gorgeous and very brilliant Georgette."

Nash warily eyeballed the dog who looked like she could easily take down Thor and stuck out his hand to the officer. "Good to meet you."

"You, too." The other man looked Nash over with the critical eye of a cop before turning back to Chelle. "Beware, my mom said she's stopping by your place for all of the gossip this afternoon."

"I'm surprised she stayed away this morning at all," Chelle said with a laugh before saying her goodbyes and heading up the stairs to the courthouse door with Nash. She glanced down at his feet with concern. "How's the ankle?"

Nash flexed the foot in question. "All better."

"I'm glad," she said, sounding as if she really had worried. Then, a second later, she grimaced as a buzz sounded from her coat. "Oh crap!" She unzipped her bright-blue puffer coat and pulled her phone out of an inside pocket. "Sorry, I have to respond to this text from the foundation board real quick."

The move gave Nash the perfect view of the upper curve of her full, pillowy tits showing above the *V* of her sweater, and his mouth went dry and his brain went blank—for all of fifteen seconds. After that, it went straight into a million naked possibilities.

Maybe sex wouldn't be such a complication. It could be a relief, an emergency relief valve, a—

Get a hold of yourself, Beckett. Chelle Finch is going to be your wife, but she's off-limits. Just stock up on lotion and you'll get through the next month just fine.

Seemingly oblivious to the gutter his thoughts were currently in, Chelle returned the phone to the inside pocket of her puffer coat and zipped it back up. "I know that was rude, I'm sorry. My uncle has the board all whipped up, and if I don't jump high enough when they reach out, then he'll use that as leverage and—" She stopped, pursed her lips together, and let out a huff of frustrated breath. "Not that any of that is important enough to air out. Again, I'm sorry."

"If it bothers you, then it is important. You know, I deal with boards all the time. What you want to do is—"

"Not be mansplained," she said, cutting him off. Grinning, she curled a finger at him, a nervous flush turning her cheeks pink. "Come on, Cucciolo, let's go get our marriage license."

There it was. She was calling him puppy again, this time in Italian. And what was he doing? Following her into the courthouse like it was the most natural thing to do to let someone else take care of things.

Nothing about this was going how he thought it would. As soon as they got the license, he'd get back in control of the situation.

How hard could that be? All of this was his idea. His plan. His solution. *She* needed *his* help.

And yet here *he* was following *her.*

The idea of not being the one controlling everything and maneuvering the people around him like pieces on a chessboard slowed his steps for a second, and she beat him to the courthouse door, pulling it open.

She held the door for him. "After you."

"No," he said, his feet rooted to the spot. "You first, I insist."

"But I'm in charge, remember?" she asked, leaning in close, her soft breath tickling his ear and sending a shot of lust straight to his balls. "That's part of the makeover. You have to do what I say."

His dick thickened against his thigh, his pulse hit the gas, and a million dirty ideas ran through his head at the same time. Just how much he liked the idea of not being in charge hit him harder than a Mack truck going eighty on the interstate.

What the hell, Beckett? That is not *how you roll. Who are you right now?*

He had no answer to that, to any of it, really. He'd started all this, but for the first time in his life, he was already in over his head—and, fuck him, his cock liked the idea very, very much.

Chapter Seven

CHELLE

"I don't know what you're talking about," Chelle hiss-whispered to her best friend. "I'm not hiding."

She was back at her apartment, marriage license hanging up on the SubZero fridge with a magnet from her vet's office. Her bestie, Karmel Kane, had been about to walk into her apartment across the hall—which was actually three apartments renovated into one massive place—when she'd spotted Chelle and Nash coming down the hall. It took the other woman all of fifteen seconds to find out they just gotten their marriage license. After that, Karmel had relocked her door and all but shoved Chelle into her own apartment, through the living room (where she'd told Nash to cool his heels in the way only a person who was definitely a dowager duchess in a past life could), and into the kitchen to get the full story.

Now Karmel was accusing her of hiding?

"You are so full of shit," Karmel said, pouring water

into a crystal wineglass and adding a thin slice of lemon and another of lime. "You are most assuredly hiding from your soon-to-be temporary husband, honey."

"I am not." Chelle made a face at her nosy neighbor turned book buddy turned closest friend and flipped her off. "I'm in here talking to you at your insistence."

Unfazed, Karmel peeked around the arched doorway leading to the living room, where Nash was, and made an appreciative mmmmm-hmmmm sound before turning her attention back to Chelle. "Yeah, and if I'd had that man in my living room right after we'd gotten our wedding license, I wouldn't have even slowed down on the way to my front door let alone allowed anyone in and then walked them into my kitchen for a little girl talk."

That was not at all how she and Karmel had ended up in her tiny Harbor City apartment kitchen, but it was no use arguing once Karmel had made up her mind.

Chelle peeked around the corner and sucked in a quick breath. Nash was down on the floor, playing with the dogs, while Sir Hiss watched from his favorite perch on the bookshelf. That was sweet, but it wasn't the three-way game of tug that had her pulse kicking up. The man had Captain America's ass, and it was temptation in its full, squeezable, smackable form.

Ignoring Karmel's knowing chuckle, Chelle turned back to her friend and asked, "Do you even know where your kitchen is?"

"Of course." She shrugged in that grand dame of stage and screen way she had and modulated her voice from Harbor City native to the vaguely somewhere in Europe accent she used for work. "It's where I store my serums and the infant blood I bathe in to keep my youthful appearance so my roles don't dry up completely." Karmel pressed the back of her hand to the underside of her chin and lifted just enough to tilt her face upward. "No one hates a woman of a certain age like Hollywood."

That last part was true, even if the baby plasma part wasn't.

"Seriously, though," Karmel continued as she relaxed back into the real her and not the one people saw in entertainment interviews, "he is delicious. I could gobble him right up."

"He's a baby," Chelle said, pushing back the very adult thoughts she'd had a minute ago. "A very hot, incredibly sexy, too young for me guy."

Karmel scoffed. "He may be a mere bambino compared to me, but you're what, a few years older than he is?"

"I'm eight years older." She knew for sure because she'd peeked at his driver's license when he'd shown it at the courthouse. That was an eon in years between an older woman and a younger man. An older guy with a younger woman? Barely a blink—even if he had a paunch and more gray hair than black.

Meanwhile, she had the kind of padding a woman got after spending more than four decades on this planet and not giving in to the people insisting on no carbs. Give up bagels when she lived in the city for the toasted delight? Yeah, that wasn't gonna happen, no matter how many times her former doctor gave her "the look" when he reviewed her weight at appointments for things like strep throat and a fractured ankle. That plushy insulation along with the lines in her forehead and droop to her formidable boobs meant to society she had entered crone territory.

Guys like Nash Beckett didn't date old ladies who looked like her—unless they wanted to win a bet.

"Age is just a number," her friend said with a wry chuckle.

"Yeah?" Chelle said. "Tell that to your agent."

Karmel let out an exaggerated stage gasp and pressed

her palm to her chest. "Stan knows I'm fifty-nine. He's the one who came up with the idea to fudge my real age in the first place. Otherwise I would have been playing middle-aged aunties and moms at thirty instead of forty-five."

"Fuck the bastards," Chelle said, clinking her own water glass against Karmel's. "But not literally, because they don't deserve us."

"Honey, so few do." She lifted her glass. "To us."

They drank to their age and fabulousness, but when Karmel put her wineglass of water down, her face had turned serious again.

"Not to go all mom friend on you, but what do you actually know about this guy? He could be a serial killer, and you're about to marry him and let him live in your apartment. He could be a hobo-sexual and this whole thing is an elaborate grift."

"He's not a hobo-sexual. He has his own house. Six of them, in fact." One of them was actually a private island, and discovering that had made Chelle actually think about staying married long enough to go on vacation. "I hired Tony Falcon to do a background check on the quick and look into him. Nash Beckett came out clean. No priors. No history of unsavory things. No current wife. No unpaid debts to the mob. No insider trading. He is pretty much exactly as he presents."

Karmel sighed and shook her head. "If you're sure."

Chelle gave her worried friend a quick hug. "I am."

"Then I'm excited for the wedding." Karmel grabbed the stack of the Guild Hunter series books by Nalini Singh from the counter, dropped them into her My Weekend's All Booked tote, and slung it over one shoulder. "Okay, I've let you hide long enough. It's time to break out of your rut and go talk to that fine man."

"It's not about that." Chelle liked being on her own, not to mention she very much did not want someone else leaving her shower curtain open or loading the dishwasher wrong, nor did she want to deal with the small annoyances that came with sharing a space with another person. Set in her ways? Hell yes, she was, and that was just fine by her. "You know how much work goes into having a husband. I've reached a point in my life when I'm happy and don't want to change anything. Getting married for real is pretty much the last thing in the world I want." Chelle set her mug down on the counter. "That's not a rut."

"No," Karmel said, "it's clinging to control because you don't want to be vulnerable because of your toxic family." She gave Chelle a quick, solid hug. "As the great line goes, life's a banquet and most poor suckers are starving to death. Go out there to that man and make yourself a plate."

"You're such a pain in my butt," Chelle grumbled even as she knew her friend was right.

"That's what makes me such a great friend."

It was exactly the opening Chelle had been waiting for. "A good enough friend to marry us tomorrow?"

"Yes!" Karmel's smile lit up her entire face. "I didn't think I'd get to do it again after Darrell and Buzz's wedding." She clapped her hands together. "Oh, this is going to be wonderful. I have to tell you, though, that I have a one hundred percent totally in love record on my weddings."

"You've only presided over your son's wedding to his fabulous husband that he already loved."

"Small details." Karmel waved off what she obviously considered minor. "Now walk me to the door. You're not going to get your happily ever after in your kitchen."

"I have an entire gallon Ziploc bag full of Twizzlers. Of course my happily ever after is here."

"A woman can't live on Twizzlers alone," Karmel said with all the gravity she'd brought to her role as an eternal fairy queen in a book adaptation that had broken box office records.

Chelle shrugged. "Well, since it's the only non-pet food in my kitchen at the moment, it'll have to do until my grocery order arrives tonight."

Karmel rolled her eyes, tucked Chelle's arm into the crook of her elbow, and walked her out into the living room, where she said a quick goodbye to Nash, blew kisses to the dogs, and closed the front door behind her fast enough that it was like Groucho and Mary were nipping at her ankles.

When Chelle turned around, Nash was sitting on the floor, with Groucho laying on his back, getting tummy pets from Nash, while Mary was snoring on the floor, tucked up against Nash's strong thigh. They say dogs always know when someone is a good person. That may or may not be true, but beyond Nash's tendency to mansplain his way onto her very last nerve, there wasn't anything about Nash Beckett that screamed "red flag."

Of course, being a good person wasn't the same as being someone she should bang—no matter what Karmel would say to that.

Nash stood up. "I have to get back to the office. Dixon and Griff will send out a search party if I'm not back for our weekly meeting."

Yeah. That reminded her… "What are you going to tell your family about our situation?"

"The truth." He started toward the door, and she fell in step beside him, their strides matching as if he'd adjusted his to be in line with her shorter one. "We're doing each other a favor."

Walking next to him set off the same sense of awareness of him as she'd had at the park, a kind of anticipation that made her breath quicken. "That's all this is."

"Exactly." He nodded.

"There's no mixing of bank accounts or fine china." Or

noticing the way his forearms looked with his shirt cuffs rolled up. "No registering for wedding gifts at Dylan's Department Store." Or refreshing her lingerie drawer. "You'll stay in the guest room, and I'll remain in my room."

They stopped by the front door, and it took everything she had to keep her face neutral, when all she could think about were all the things that weren't going to happen because, just like her books, this wasn't real life.

"We'll have to go out on six dates planned by my cousins." He reached out and pushed a strand of the hair framing her face, tucking it behind her ear, an intense look on his face that sent a shiver across her skin.

"Is that part of the bet?" she asked, sounding as breathless as if she'd just climbed to the top of some distant mountain and then jogged back to Harbor City. "Six dates and nothing else?"

No kissing. No touching. No sex. No waking up the next morning with his hard cock pressed against her ass. Just a nice, normal, completely platonic, temporary alliance of the marital variety.

"Nothing else—except for my mansplainer makeover." His jaw tightened and his gaze dropped to her mouth. "When I do what you say."

Did his voice get a little bit of a growl in it when he mentioned makeover? It had to be her imagination, her writer brain putting that lust in his eye, the knowing grin on his lips, and the cocky, almost asking for trouble vibe in his stance.

Michelle Finch, stop right there. He is a puppy. Focus.

Trying to regain her equilibrium, she took a step back and smoothed any expression from her face, forcing it into a neutrality she definitely did not feel inside. "We can start that after the wedding."

"Whatever you say." He winked at her and opened her front door but didn't walk through. "I ordered you lunch from the deli around the corner. It should be delivered here any minute."

"Why would you do that?" she asked, too shocked to self-censor or go with the more polite thank-you.

"I overheard you saying the only food you had was a cabinet full of Twizzlers."

Everything she and Karmel had said about him ran at triple speed through her head. Embarrassment rushed up from her toes in a hot whoosh. "Is that *all* you heard?"

He grinned at her, his dimples in both cheeks going deep. "Not even close. And just for the record, I think older women are sexy as hell."

And then he turned and was gone, but the hot tension low in her belly and palpable sense of anticipation remained.

Her soon-to-be husband was the last man she should be thinking about naked. And yet, here she was wondering if she had enough time to get off before her lunch arrived.

Chapter Eight

NASH

December 2nd...

Some people got wedding day jitters. Not Nash.

Marrying Chelle Finch was the most efficient way to get what they both wanted. It was as simple as that.

Of course, that didn't mean everything wasn't total fucking chaos in Chelle's apartment today, thanks to the combination of animals and his cousins.

Chelle's cat was on top of the bookshelf in the living room, taking whacks at anyone who got a little too close to its lair—which was exactly why Nash had made sure to tell his cousin Dixon to stand there. Nash would pay for that later, no doubt, but it was worth it to watch his cousin jump a foot in the air in surprise when Sir Hiss had given him a quick one-two thwack.

Then there were the dogs that were shut in Chelle's room with her as she got ready for her walk down the aisle, but barking their heads off because the living room was filled with Becketts talking loud, trying to coax the cat down, and offering Nash pre-wedding advice he didn't need because this was an arrangement, not a forever. He'd managed to ditch them all—at least as much as he could in a packed living room—when his mom started sharing memories of her wedding night.

There wasn't enough bleach in the world to erase that from his brain, and just as horrible Dixon and Griff were headed right toward him, looking exactly like they had that time when they were twelve and triple-dog dared him into spending the night in the supposedly haunted tower at Gable House. Nash had no idea what those two were up to now, but he knew it wasn't going to be good. Thank fuck, he was saved when Chelle's friend Karmel clapped her hands.

"If I can have everyone's attention," she said as she made her way over to the fireplace, where the ceremony would take place. "The show is about to start."

While everyone settled into their chairs arranged so there was an aisle that led from Chelle's bedroom door to the hearth, Nash took his place up front, next to Karmel. Chelle's friend was wearing what looked like a vicar's costume from some British TV show where there was a grizzly murder every episode, and he couldn't help but think that Grandma Betty would have approved. She was a woman who liked making a statement.

"You know," Karmel said, keeping her voice low so that only he could hear. "They say that when a woman gets to a certain point in her life, she stops having one-night stands and instead has auditions. Just something to keep in mind when you turn around to see your bride."

She pressed the play button on her phone, and the wedding march started playing through the Bluetooth speaker. Nash didn't bother to wait to turn around. Looking past his family, he sucked in a breath when he saw Chelle standing in the open doorway, flanked by her pugs who were in doggie formal wear. Chelle had skipped the veil and had left her dark hair down. Her pale-pink lace dress clung to her curves and stopped just below her knees. That was all it took for Nash to start to wonder how in the hell he could get an audition.

The pugs pranced around her feet as Chelle walked up the aisle, making their crystal-encrusted leashes sparkle in the sunlight coming in through the apartment's big windows. By the time she got all the way up the aisle to stand next to him, the dogs had circled their leashes around her calves enough that she was taking tiny little steps.

"I know how that feels," he said as he knelt down and unwound the leashes from her legs while the pugs gave excited yips and yaps in-between delivering happy kisses to his face. "There, got you."

When he glanced up at her from his position, his fingers still brushing the sides of her calves, he could have sworn he heard a crack of thunder, but the sky outside was bright the way only a cloudless December sky could be.

"You know there are training techniques you can use to get them to walk on an assigned side of you," he said, the words coming out even as he could feel his entire family wince behind him—and, in fact, heard several of them groan. "The key is to hold the lead so that—"

"Nash," Chelle said, cutting him off. "We'll talk about it later."

The rest of the wedding ceremony went by fast, and before he knew it, he had a simple gold band on his finger, and she had a matching one on hers.

"If anyone objects to the marriage, speak now or forever hold your peace," Karmel said, pausing for a moment before opening her mouth to continue.

"I object," a man called out from the back of the apartment.

Every head in the room turned as if on a synchronized swivel to look where a scrawny guy in a huge cowboy hat stood in the doorway.

"Uncle Buckley," Chelle said, her entire body practically vibrating with fury. "You weren't invited, and you aren't supposed to have a key to this place."

This was her asshole uncle? The man had the perpetual shithead vibe to him that made it seem plausible that his hobbies were pulling the wings off of flies and telling small children that Santa Claus was fake. His narrow-eyed gaze focused on Chelle with an intensity that made Nash take a step forward to put his body between hers and her uncle's as Groucho and Mary growled at Chelle's feet, the fur on their backs going up in spikes.

"Yeah, well, you're supposed to be honoring your father's will, not making a farce of it," Buckley said. "That's why I object."

"On what grounds?" Karmel asked, annoyance dripping from her tone.

"Because all of this is a joke," Buckley said, spittle flying from his lips. "There's no way anyone would think of you as an eligible bride."

"Why the hell not?" Nash asked, the words coming out before he realized he was going to say anything.

"Look at her," Buckley spluttered. "She's too old to have kids. She's fat. She's weird."

Everything inside Nash went absolutely still, and his vision narrowed down to the point that all he could see was that dipshit's bulbous nose. The one he was going to go break—maybe in more than one place.

"One, I don't want kids," Nash said, his fury rising with each word. "Two, she's fucking gorgeous. Three, a person is either weird or an asshole, and we all know where you fall on that spectrum."

While Chelle's uncle practically spit he was so mad, Nash was walking toward the asshole before he even realized he was moving. However, Chelle's hand on his arm stopped him, pulling his attention away from the shitbird and to the way the gold band on her ring finger glinted in the sun. Then he looked up at his wife. Her jaw was tight and her eyes suspiciously watery.

Nash had never wanted to commit murder more in his life.

"Please don't," she said, her voice barely above a whisper. "He's not worth it."

Something inside Nash snapped in that moment. It was so sharp, so intense, that he heard a crack like a tree branch getting hit by lightning and shattering.

He didn't think.

He didn't consider.

He just pivoted, cupped Chelle's face in his hands, and kissed her.

It started out for show, a fuck-you to her uncle and his asshat objection, but it didn't stay that way. Sometime in the second between his lips touching hers and his tongue sweeping across the seam of her mouth, everything changed. It morphed from a declaration to a plea, from a protective action to a promise, from a spur-of-the-moment impulse to a need that went marrow deep.

Chelle let out a low moan as she melted against his chest and opened up for him. He didn't hesitate. There was no way he could have. It felt too perfect with her lush body pressed against him and her fingers gripping his suit lapels as if she needed to hold on or she'd get sucked under by the same unexpected wave of lust that had him ready to strip naked right here and right now.

It wasn't until he felt a tap on his shoulder that he pulled back.

"The dogs scared the shit out of that knobhead before your cousins scooped them up. Then your uncle ran his little fake cowboy ass out the door," Karmel said, sounding bloodthirsty and slightly disappointed in that outcome. "So if you two want to go ahead with the ceremony to make this whole marriage thing official, you should stop making out now. Some people looked uncomfortable about seeing that kiss. I mean, I thought it was hot as hell, but you should probably go ahead and finish the I-dos."

Which was exactly what they did—or at least that was his assumption, because the rest of the ceremony went by in a blur. She said words. He said words. They showed their phones to prove that she'd responded to his Bramble bio. Now they were on opposite ends of her non-efficiently arranged living room, with her charming the shit out of Griff and his fiancée, Kinsey, without even glancing his way, while Nash couldn't stop watching her. All he could think about was that kiss and how good Chelle had felt, all of her soft curves pressed up against him. And that little moan she'd made? He'd be hearing that tonight when he had his hand curled around his dick.

Alone.

Because this marriage wasn't real.

Well, they were legally bound together, but this wasn't a marriage in the true sense. Just two people coming together for mutual orgasms.

No!

For mutual benefit.

For fuck's sake, Nash, get your shit together.

"Oh, honey," his mom said, slipping her arm through his and laying her head on his shoulder. "I knew you two would be perfect for each other."

"Mom," he said, reminding himself of the truth almost as much as his mother. "It's a transactional situation."

She let out a dramatic gasp—the same one she used when she was shocked, *shocked*, her cell phone bill had to be paid every month—and took a step back. "Then why did you kiss her like that?"

"Because I'm not a total asshole like her uncle." And it was better than punching the old geezer in the face even though he'd deserved it.

"You know, for someone who thinks he knows everything, you sure don't know yourself." She gave one of those headshakes of disappointment that only moms made. "But don't worry, the universe knows, honey. I'm sure you boys will figure out some other way to determine who should get your grandma's last present."

"It'll be mine because I'm going to win that bet," he said, unable to stop watching his wife as she went from one of his overwhelming family members to the other seemingly totally at ease. "I am not going to fall in love with Chelle Finch."

He had no doubts.

He was right about this.

He was *always* right.

"Of course not, honey." His mom patted his cheek hard enough to border on a smack. "I don't doubt it for a second."

Nash knew his mom was humoring him, but he wasn't kidding. His was going to be one of the countless loveless marriages out there.

His plan was perfect. He had absolutely nothing to worry about.

Chapter Nine

Somehow Chelle's lips still tingled from that kiss.

It was hours after she'd said, "I do." Thirty minutes had passed since the last guest left. Minutes ago, she'd taken off her wedding dress and had put on her ultra-moisturizing under-eye patches. Then she'd followed that up by shoving her hair into a half-assed bun that skipped messy and went straight into just survived a hurricane.

Still, she couldn't get that kiss out of her head.

No one—absolutely no one—had ever kissed her like that before. It was as if Nash wanted to wipe her memory of every other man she'd ever been with. It had been amazing and she wanted more. Of course, she couldn't have more, because it had been a pity kiss meant to shut up her asshole of an uncle.

And yet...

Butterflies were doing synchronized loop-de-loops in her stomach, and she stopped in the middle of buttoning up the pajama shirt that matched her black-and-white dragon pajama pants and brought her fingertips to her lips. Closing her eyes, she gave in to the sizzle that had her whole body a little trembly and put herself back in that moment as music poured in through her earbuds.

They hadn't had a first dance. Instead, after the ceremony, they'd had a very civilized cocktail party—if she didn't count the fact that Sir Hiss had spent the whole time stalking Nash's cousin Dixon as if he had pockets full of catnip treats. Then everyone had gone home and she'd gone into hiding.

Okay. She'd told Nash she needed a bath to recharge and then a book to unwind before she could even think about talking to another human being ever again, but they both knew she was running away because she had no idea what to do with the man staying in her guest room for the next month.

She'd figure out the answer to that tomorrow. Tonight, she was going to forget about that kiss. Somehow. Someway. She'd figure it out.

"Fuck!"

Nash's curse came through over the *Game of Thrones* soundtrack (don't get her started on that last season) and she yanked out one of her earbuds. It took her a second to work out what the scraping and soft thumps coming from the living room meant, but when she did, she marched over to her bedroom door and flung it open.

That.

Giant.

Prick.

He thought he could ignore her and rearrange her life as if her wishes didn't even matter? No effing way. She'd lived through that already. It wasn't going to happen again. Ever.

Was she hyping herself up for exactly what she spent her entire real life avoiding—confrontation? Fuck yes, she was— she had to.

She could do it.

She could do it.

She could do it.

She repeated her mantra in her head as she walked down the hall, the pugs sprinting ahead of her into the living room, eager to investigate the noise. If she was the heroine in one of her books, she would have a fire-and-brimstone-worthy ass chewing already coming together in her mind like the perfect scene in one of her books. Too bad this was real life and she was just a human woman who was trying to learn new habits in her forties—exactly when every part of her wanted her to stay in her comfort zone. What she wouldn't do to have a flaming sword or the acid venom her nymph assassins always carried instead of a shaky inner voice talking to her like she was a train in a kids' book.

The words of her mantra scattered like cockroaches when the lights came on, though, the moment she walked through the curved archway dividing her living room from the hallway. She whacked her shin on the corner of the coffee table and stopped dead in her tracks—but not because of the pain.

No, she jolted to a halt because of what she saw.

There in the middle of her living room (where the couch was now in the wrong place even if it did look better there) Nash stood shirtless in a pair of low-slung gray sweatpants. His sleepwear gave just enough of a hint as to what he was packing beneath them in commando form to make her mouth go dry and her nipples tighten into hard points.

She could do him.

Shut up, brain! That is not the mantra!

His abs and biceps weren't chiseled like a guy who spent every spare moment of his day either in the gym, working out, or pounding protein shakes. No. Instead of having the show muscles of a gym bro, he had a hard-as-fuck tank of a bod with a solid chest, thick, strong arms, and powerful shoulders. It was like looking up and finding that she was on the shirtless, burly, blue-collar lumberjack side of TikTok or something. And she was soooooooo here for it—or at least she would be if she didn't remember at that moment that she was supposed to be annoyed enough to go nymph assassin on his very fine ass.

"What are you doing?" she asked once she found her voice and got her eyes to focus on his face, instead of appreciating how his high, round ass kept those gray sweatpants in place.

Nash squatted down and pet the dogs, who were all bug-eyed in love with him. "Fixing things."

"Excuse me?"

"It was all wrong." He stood up, crossing his arms and bracing his legs as if he was ready for a battle. "But don't worry, I'm fixing it. How you had it really messed with the traffic flow of the room. Plus, I noticed after the wedding that Sir Hiss didn't have a no-dog-zone climbing spot after the bookshelves. However, if they bracket the big window like this, he can go from one to the couch to the other and then take the fireplace mantle to the chair, and then *bam*, he's made the circle to the third bookshelf in its original spot."

"That could be the case," she said, not liking that she had to admit (only to herself, thank you very much) that he was right about that, along with moving the couch over a bit that way and the chair nudged a few feet this way. "But I liked it the way it was."

"And I saw how you hit your shin on the coffee table three times today because it's in an awkward space," he countered, his gaze going over her body as if he was memorizing it for later.

"The room was filled to the gills with your family." She fought to keep her hand from going to that third button on her shirt and closing it. Usually, she was alone, so there wasn't anyone to guard from getting a large flash of cleavage. The girls needed to air out after a day spent locked in an underwire prison. Nighttime was their time to be free. "Normally, I don't have anyone here."

"Really?" He lifted an eyebrow. "You did it when you walked in here just now."

Fuck. Way to go, Michelle.

"I was distracted," she said, fumbling for an answer that didn't make her sound totally inept.

"By what?" he asked, clearly knowing the answer already.

She should have shot back a response, but then he put his hands on his hips, the move edging the waistband of his gray sweatpants down another inch or two. Maybe she was looking really hard or maybe the light coming in from the streetlamps was just right for her to notice the dusting of light brown hair on his chest and the slightly darker line of hair that disappeared beneath his waistband. She needed to drag her gaze upward. Logically, she knew this was true. She only made it as far as his bare chest before getting stuck there.

If she was a character in one of her books, this would be a sign that a spell had been cast and that she needed to watch out. However, she was not a nymph in one of her fantasy stories. She was a woman in her forties with a BMI that made her doctor give her the side-eye, in a short-term marriage of convenience with a guy she barely knew.

This wasn't real life. It sure as hell wasn't the beginning of a real marriage (AKA death by gold band).

She'd seen what happened to the women who went into marriage fresh and optimistic and walked away tired, worn, and cynical. Even if this *wasn't* a fictional marriage, she had decided she was too old and set in her ways to let a man mess with her shit. For once in her life, she was going to put her foot down. She wouldn't go with the flow. She wouldn't just accept that this was the way things had to be. She was going to take a page from her characters' book and be a badass.

Kinda.

Sorta.

Okay, this was her first test, and she wouldn't fail in sticking up for doing things her way just because a half-naked Nash made her breath catch and her heart speed up.

"Oh," he said, taking a few steps closer. "Were you distracted by *me*?"

He came to a stop only a few feet from her, and she couldn't help but notice that pale freckles dotted his broad shoulders and cascaded down until they were hidden by his chest hair.

The satyrs in her books should definitely have more freckles.

She let out a shaky breath as a sense of uber-awareness of Nash washed over her and pocketed the image for later—yes, she was a weak person.

"Not in the least." Why did her voice sound so squeaky all of the sudden? "I was worried about your ankle."

"It's all better today." He balanced all of his weight on his right foot for a few seconds before putting his left foot back down. "And anyway, that answer didn't sound anything like the truth."

Because it was a gigantic lie.

Okay, if her heart could stop fluttering like that for half a second, she could come up with something to distract him with. She was the queen of winging it when writing her books. This should be easy. All she had to do was think of Nash as the annoying satyr with freckles on his shoulders and she'd be fine.

Okay, brain, any minute now.

No, don't look down at the outline of his dick again.

ACK! Not at his broad chest, either.

His face—nope that's not gonna work, either.

Okay, that spot on the wall to the left of his ear. Perfect. That's the one. Now, do your magic thing, brain.

Thank God, it did.

"I don't care what it sounded like," she said, dialing into

that dismissive tone her dad had used with her for her entire life that didn't, not even a little bit, sound like it should be coming out of her mouth. "But since I'm up, we might as well work out the details for how we're going to do this for the next month. Number one, no moving my furniture around."

He looked around the chaos that was once her everything-in-its-place living room. "Fine."

"And we each stick to our own space within the apartment." She drew an invisible line in the air with her finger, dividing the room in two. That part of her apartment was his dance space and over here would be hers. "That shouldn't be hard, since you'll be at Beckett Cosmetics all day and I like to read in bed at night."

He shook his head. "No."

"What, now you're trying to tell me I can't read in bed?" She planted her hands on her hips and glared at Nash. There was no way, not after growing up with the book police yanking any book that even hinted of a world where people rebelled against authority. She didn't have a lot of lines that were labeled *do not cross*, but that was for sure one of them. "Do you have some bullshit mansplaining spiel about shit-erature and how it gives people unrealistic expectations about life and how people should treat them?"

"I meant the me going to the office part." He shoved his hands in the pockets of his sweatpants and rocked back on his heels, managing to look like some kind of bashful thirst trap. "We allow our staff to work from home, if they want, from Thanksgiving to after New Year's so everyone can have some extra downtime around the holidays. As the top three executives in the company, my cousins and I lead by example. I haven't been in the office after turkey day in five years."

Chelle's jaw dropped. "You've got to be kidding me."

A whole month of this? There weren't enough batteries. Her fingers were going to get whatever the knuckle version of lockjaw was.

"So you're going to be here all the time?" she asked, pressing her hand to the base of her neck, where her pulse was going fast enough to break a land-speed record.

Nash grinned at her, showing off the double dimples of disaster for her panties. "Pretty much."

Oh God.

This couldn't get worse.

Beyond the epic levels of horniness he inspired, how in the hell was she supposed to get any writing done?

She had a system, a process. It involved everyone in the world leaving her the fuck alone, and it was glorious. She did foundation work in the afternoon, but the mornings were reserved for fighting magical evil, thrilling side quests, and stand-in-front-of-the-open-freezer sex scenes.

How in the hell was she supposed to focus with Nash around all the time?

"You won't even know I'm here," he said.

The low timbre of his voice danced along her skin, teasing her senses and giving her all sorts of ideas that she had no business having about her temporary husband.

"I seriously doubt that," she said as she headed back to her room, Groucho and Mary prancing along at her heels.

"Chelle," he called out.

She stopped and turned. "Yes?"

"About that kiss." He looked her in the eyes, holding her gaze and locking her in place. "I'm sorry. I shouldn't have done that."

"It was nothing." She clenched her hands to keep from touching her lips again. "I'd already forgotten all about it." How she didn't just burst into you're-a-big-liar flames on the spot she had no clue. She really was too old to be this turned on by a pity kiss. Fuck. Time to get back to familiar ground, and a normal living room. She took a deep breath, girded her loins, and let it rip. "Please put all of my furniture back."

"Yes, ma'am." He tipped his chin but didn't bother to smother the teasing grin on his face. "One question. What about the coffee table? Another six inches that way and you won't be in danger of hitting it."

She blinked in confusion as her head spun at his personality transplant. "Are you...asking my permission?"

Why did she sound so confused about that? It was definitely stated as a question, but...no one ever really asked her anything. Even at the foundation she just took orders from the board and did her best to take their limited vision and help as many people as possible. No one asked what she thought or if she knew how they could do things better or her opinion or for her *permission*.

"I am." Something intense flashed in his eyes as his gaze went from her mouth down to the deep *V* of her not-closed-all-the-way pajama top, and his dimples deepened as if he knew exactly what he was doing to her at that moment. "I should do that as part of the don't-be-a-mansplaining-asshole lessons, right?"

Hot, slick desire rushed through her before she could even try to squash it. All she could do was remind herself that Nash Becket was not for her. He was cocky and full of himself and a know-it-all. He was the last man she could or should ever want.

Too bad, you do anyway.

Shut up, brain.

"Fine," she said, starting for her door again before she combusted right in front of him. "Put the coffee table where you want."

And then she shut the door to her room and went straight for the shower, because she was a woman who needed to cover her body in ice water to get a mansplainer out of her head before she did something even more foolish than marrying him.

Chapter Ten

This was not how Nash had imagined he'd be spending his wedding night—not that he'd ever spent much time thinking about it. However, he'd always believed that if the worst had happened and he'd actually gotten married, then he'd spend the night having sex with his wife.

Instead, here he was moving furniture to put everything—well, almost everything—back in the bad arrangement it had been in before he started. Except this time, he had a raging hard-on and absolutely no hope of finding relief for it with his bride. It was bad enough before she'd come out of her room. But one look at her in those shouldn't-have-been-sexy-as-hell pajamas with her hair all messed up like she'd just been rolling around in the bed had made it so much worse.

Fuck.

Maybe he'd been wrong about the brilliance of his plan to get married to win the bet.

Or maybe you just need to get your wife out of your system.

He stopped mid-shove as he moved the bookcases back into position, processing what the voice in the back of his head had whispered. No, there was no way that wouldn't complicate things. His life had enough complications already. He had his parents to keep on the straight and narrow, his siblings to advise, deals to make to grow Beckett Cosmetics, and the Last Man Standing bet to finish, with Grandma's present to unwrap when he won. There was a reason why he didn't even have a goldfish at his house.

He rubbed his palm against the back of his neck, shook the stupid idea out of his head, and pushed the bookcase back to the very wrong spot for this space.

Still, he kept picturing the way Chelle had looked at him when she'd first walked out of her bedroom. There was surprise, which was expected considering it was after midnight. Then there had been appraisal, and then there'd been lust. She'd shut it down pretty quickly, but not before he'd caught it.

Chelle was interested.

And he was more than interested in her.

Really, what could go wrong with a limited-time agreement for mutual orgasms?

He picked up the ottoman and carried it over to its spot to the side of the archway as Sir Hiss supervised his progress from on top of the fireplace mantle.

Nash couldn't shake the idea that sleeping with his wife just might be the best way for them to get through the next month. They'd scratch the itch, and all of that tension would ease. It could be as simple as that.

No complications.

No strings.

By the time Nash had moved the rest of the furniture back into place and then adjusted the placement of the coffee table to six inches off from the original spot, he'd made up his mind to seduce his wife.

Chapter Eleven

CHELLE

Chelle was gonna be a widow before Christmas.

Nash hadn't stopped talking for the past two hours. He'd paced the living room while on a call with business associates in London, taken four calls from his mom to walk her through restarting her internet router, and had a long conversation with Sir Hiss about why the cat couldn't walk across the counters in the kitchen.

Okay, the last one had been funny because the cat had spent the entire time purring and rubbing up against Nash who was—thankfully—fully dressed today.

Yeah, she'd peeked when refilling on coffee and Twizzlers. Sue her.

She'd written approximately one hundred words in her book (goal two thousand) if she didn't count the number of Beckett Cosmetics–related sales calls she'd accidentally transcribed into dialogue for her formerly taciturn hero who couldn't seem to shut up now. That had been bad enough, but

Nash had DoorDashed what smelled like charbroiled heaven in food form and was right now having a conversation about the delivery guy's killer sneakers and how he had customized them. Nash was just starting to offer unsolicited advice on color combinations and marketing focus groups when Chelle hurried out of her room before she got put on some DoorDash pain-in-the-ass blacklist.

By the time she got to her front door, with the pugs chasing her, yapping excitedly at whatever game was being played, the delivery guy had that pinched expression of someone who wanted to be somewhere—anywhere—else.

"Nash," she said through a strained smile.

He turned, his smile going two-dimples deep when he spotted her. "Hey, ready for a lunch break?"

"Sure. Awesome. Yes." Anything to rescue the delivery guy who didn't even stick around long enough to say goodbye before he high-tailed it away from her apartment.

Chelle shut the door and leaned her back against it as she let out a long sigh.

For his part, Nash stayed where he was, standing in the middle of the little hall that made up her foyer. She shouldn't notice that the blue of his sweater that spanned his broad chest matched the blue in his eyes, or the fact that his jeans were doing God's work, highlighting the absolute, stone-cold solid thickness of his thighs. The man was just big and solid, like a giant stack of doorstopper books come to life—but one holding two delicious-smelling bags and grinning at her as if she was the cherry on the extra whipped cream topping of his Oreo shake.

A hot flash of tingly lust blasted up from the center of her black leggings, and her mouth went dry as he watched her.

Good Lord. This man discombobulated her. He had her all jittery and thinking inappropriate thoughts about her husband who wasn't her husband but kinda was and—

My God, Chelle! Simmer down on the spiral before you just rip off your clothes right here and now.

Pulling back from the edge, she turned and flipped the locks on her front door, then put the chain on. "You can't do that."

"Do what?" He unrolled the top of one of the brown bags he was holding and took a deep inhale before closing his eyes and letting out a low groan of appreciation.

Her brain went offline for a second at the sound.

Really, it should be illegal to make that noise that had her wondering if that's the sound he'd make while between her legs.

Clearing her throat, she tore her gaze away from him and rebooted her brain, digging for the just-go-with-the-flow version of herself that she was determined to find. Somewhere. Down deep. It had to be there. Right?

Focus, Michelle!

Letting out a sigh, she pulled herself back from the brink. "You shouldn't give so much unasked-for advice."

"But it's good advice, and customized shoes are a growing market segment and—"

She silenced him with a glance that actually surprised her at her own boldness, then started down the hall toward the kitchen, because she needed some ice-cold water before she ignited from being that close to him. "Not everyone wants to turn something they love into a side hustle."

"But he had something so great," Nash said, keeping up with her in the narrow hall. "Just a little tweak here and there, and he'd be in the sweet spot."

"Nash," she said, putting all of the censure she could muster in her voice when 88 percent of her thoughts were taken up with fantasies involving him between her thighs.

He shot her a rueful grin. "This is makeover business, huh?"

Something in the rough sandpaper of his voice made her look at him as they walked through the arched entry into her kitchen with the bright canary-yellow walls she hated, and her breath caught. He was close—so close—but not touching her even though he was big enough that it had to have been an effort not to in the confined space. The fact that he had pulled back was somehow almost hotter than if he actually was touching her.

Oh my God, Chelle. You've been alone so long that you're broken.

Hustling across the room, she got a glass out of the cabinet and filled it with ice from the fridge dispenser, fastidiously avoiding looking at him again, because that's how the bad thoughts happened. "It's the you-don't-have-to-run-everyone's-life business."

Nash stayed in the archway, leaning one shoulder against it, watching her, his gaze intense and his grip tight on the food bags. "You seem tense. Anything I can help with?"

She froze. Was that flirting? Was her fake husband *flirting* with her? He couldn't be. There was just no way a hot billionaire like Nash Beckett would flirt with a woman eight years older than him, with enough gray in her hair that her stylist had gone from calling it nature's glitter to saying Chelle had earned her stripes.

She was so discombobulated—again—by the possibility that her husband just maybe thought about her naked that she blurted out a truth, if not *the* truth. "It's the color of the kitchen that makes me tense. I hate it, but when my aunt left me the apartment, her will stipulated I couldn't repaint the kitchen."

"Your family has a tradition of weirdly controlling wills," Nash said.

"Yeah," she said with a chuckle that was about 75 percent awkward nerves. "It's definitely a quirk."

"Well, does the paint color mean you don't want lunch in here?"

"Depends," she said, sounding way more calm than she felt at the moment. "What is it?"

One side of his mouth lifted in a smirk that promised he'd already won. "The best cheeseburger you've ever tasted in your life."

Ugh. That wasn't fair. Considering her totally crappy work progress for the day, it was definitely a cheeseburger day and ketchup delivered via crinkle-cut fries kind of day. "Are there fries?"

He opened one of the brown paper bags, this one with grease stains on the bottom corner—always a good sign—and revealed a large red-striped paper cup overflowing with golden-brown deep-fried potatoes begging to be dragged through a vast sea of ketchup.

She inhaled, and all of her happy responses kicked into gear. Oh, she knew that seasoning mix. There was only one place in Harbor City that got the ratio right. "From Vito's Diner?"

Nash shrugged his broad shoulders. "It is the best in Harbor City."

He wasn't lying. Although they were best known for an item that wasn't in Nash's oversize hands.

"No shakes?" she teased.

"Nah." He shook his head and made his way over to the little two-person table tucked into the corner of her kitchen. "You gotta get those in person so you get the overage in the silver mixing cup."

Oh yes, the overage. It was an amazing bonus that made the divine shakes even better. "Good point."

"What?" He kept his face down, but there was no missing his smug grin as he took out the foil-wrapped cheeseburgers and then ripped the paper bag holding the fries so that it unfolded and made the perfect basket for them. "That isn't mansplaining?"

"Don't ruin the moment, Nash." Chelle tucked her water glass in the crook of her arm and took two plates out of the cabinet, then took them over to the table. "Just accept the win."

He laughed. It was a good sound, the kind of friendly, happy sound of a man who did it often. "Does that mean I get to feed you french fries while you tell me all about what you're doing in your room?"

She rolled her eyes and sat down. "It's not that interesting."

"I don't believe that," he said as he took the seat across from her.

Bracing herself for more questions, Chelle unwrapped her cheeseburger and took a bite before putting it down. Then she did her best to keep her gaze on her plate as she loaded it with fries and several large squirts of ketchup, because looking at Nash while he ate wasn't an option. Whatever a poker face was for food, he didn't have it. Instead, it was just raw appreciation for the deliciousness in his mouth. The bad ideas it gave her were delicious in a whole other way.

Fuck. They said your forties meant a whole new level of constant sexual awareness, but this was ridiculous. She was a grown-ass woman with a healthy self-care orgasm routine. The last thing she wanted was a hulk of a man disrupting her with things she couldn't have.

Luckily for her, once they started eating, the deliciousness of Vito's cheeseburgers and fries superseded conversation. If Nash thought about a more efficient way she could use her fries as edible scoops to deliver massive amounts of ketchup, he kept his mouth shut about it. They were both finishing up when his phone buzzed.

He picked it up off the table, and his face scrunched up when he looked at the screen. "Our first date is set."

Ah yes, the reason for this whole farce for him—the Last Man Standing bet. Her pulse picked up in anticipation, which was really not what she needed right now. Couldn't he just be completely unappealing? Wasn't that what everyone wanted in a fake husband?

If only her body was on board with that plan. Right now, it was waaaaaay too focused on what that date would be and if it would involve touching him. Dancing? Tandem sky diving? Couples massage? Yeah, her body had much different priorities than the rest of her.

Chapter Twelve

NASH

"You're not taking a picture of me in the shower."

Standing in the fake bathroom at the Waterbury IKEA that evening, Nash knew one thing: he was going to kill his cousins. Of course, he highly doubted Griff and Dixon thought up a photo scavenger hunt date on their own. This had Fiona's and Kinsey's fingerprints all over it. Even worse, it was a scavenger hunt of documented embarrassment with photos to prove every find.

"You're completely dressed," Chelle said. "Come on, do you want to win the scavenger hunt or not?"

And that was the question, wasn't it? He was competitive right down to the marrow of his bones, and no one knew that better than his cousins and, apparently, their fiancées.

Those fuckers.

Looking around at the fake bathroom in the middle of the absolutely ginormous IKEA showroom, Nash realized that he was going to do this. His cousins would have known that he'd eventually do that. None of the Beckett cousins would let a little momentary embarrassment get in the way of winning. The rules of the Last Man Standing bet were simple:

1. Go on six dates with the woman who is the first to answer the Bramble dating app bio.

2. Each date would be arranged by the other cousins.

3. Wake up Christmas morning not in love and be the one to get Grandma Betty's last present.

Of course, none of this was supposed to apply to him, because he'd known from the beginning that Grandma's scheme had been to get her grandchildren to quit the single life and settle down with the love of their life. And he'd kept his mouth shut about it because he knew that was the only way he'd win. That's why selling the idea of the Last Man Standing bet to his cousins had been so easy—he knew exactly what buttons to push to get Dixon and Griff to do exactly what they were dead set against. The flip side of that, of course, was that they'd known him all his life and, therefore, knew all of his weak spots, too.

The largest of which was being a total asshole in public.

"Is there really winning or is it just abject humiliation?" he grumbled as he pushed back the white vinyl shower curtain surrounding the fake shower, because yeah, he was doing this despite the fact that there were a billion people in the store.

"Tell you what," Chelle said, her lips curled into an encouraging grin. "We get all the pics to finish this scavenger hunt, and I'll buy you a beer after."

Beer in a dark booth in a dive bar with Chelle, where they had to sit thigh-to-thigh close and there was a good chance he'd get to put his arm on the back of the booth and around her? Yeah, that was definitely a reward.

"Two beers." He stepped inside the shower stall and almost fit (he could look over the shower curtain bar without trying). "I'm a big guy, and this is a small shower."

"Deal." Chelle took a few steps back and held up her phone to get the shot. "Now give me a good face."

There was no going back now. It would be less embarrassing if it weren't for the fact that what pushed him over the edge and scrunching down under the non-functioning showerhead in the teeny-tiny stall in the fake bathroom display as people streamed by was that she'd smiled at him.

"My cousins are going to use this as blackmail for the rest of my life." He'd be lucky if these shots didn't make it onto the Beckett Cosmetics website or some such shit.

Chelle rolled her eyes and squatted down to take a shot from a low angle. "Cheer up. You might get hit by a bus."

He laughed loud enough to catch the attention of the harried couple who'd spent the last ten minutes arguing by the bookcase displays. "That's not a happy thought."

"True"—she thumbed through the pictures on her phone—"but you laughed anyway."

"It's this place," he grumbled. "IKEA has made me lose my good sense."

"That's what it does," she said as she stepped closer and began closing the shower curtain a bit. "Did you know couples end up breaking up all the time after a trip here?"

"Good thing we're motivated to stay together," he said.

He glanced over at the couple that had gone back to arguing about the benefits of Billy versus Kallax bookcases. The woman's nose had turned red and the guy had crossed his arms and taken the posture of a pissed-off donkey. The urge to exit the shower so he could go mediate the strangers' disagreement and offer advice about which bookcases to get had him taking a step out of the shower before he even realized it. Really, they needed him. He could help make sure they didn't let an IKEA argument turn into a failed relationship, which would turn into a life of being lonely because they'd lost that one person who completed them.

He took another step toward the couple, but Chelle shot him a look that stopped him. Well, that and the fact that she'd put her hand on his chest, which sent a lightning bolt of lust straight to his dick.

She pulled back her hand, flexing her fingers as if she'd felt it, too. "Give folks a chance to solve their own problems."

"But—"

She tilted her chin down and shook her head. "You don't have to fix everything for everyone, Nash."

Chelle could be right.

Maybe.

Sure, there was a strong chance that she was more correct than incorrect.

Possibly.

Normally, he'd already be up in the couple's business, offering his guidance and keeping them from having to experience the painful consequences of failure, but instead he took in a deep breath and let that anxious knot at the idea of someone needing help unwind in his stomach with the exhale. By the time he was done, the couple was holding hands again and taking the pickup location cards for both types of bookcases.

Chelle could have given him a told-you-so look, but instead she took a step back and held up her phone as he got back in the shower. "Close the curtain and peek out like I just interrupted you."

Yeah, those were not the kind of ideas he needed in his head when he was in public. His dick was half hard, and he was thanking the universe for the shower curtain hanging between them.

And because the universe loved to fuck with him, she

picked that moment to sweep the curtain back. Luckily for the little bit of pride he still had at that moment, instead of looking down at his unprompted but becoming a little too common boner around her, she grabbed the removable showerhead and handed it to him.

"Now sing into the showerhead," she said as she angled her phone for the perfect shot.

And he did it. Like, he went full front man in the middle of a big arena show—he was all exaggerated facial expressions and way too into it body language, complete with the whole head thrown back showered mic above his face thing. Why? Because it made Chelle giggle, and hearing that gave him the same rush as closing a massive Beckett Cosmetics distribution deal or winning a stupid bet with his cousins.

Though, really, there was more to it. Those things always left him craving whatever came next. This? He just wanted to bask in the light sound of her enjoyment of him making an ass of himself.

"Why am I doing this again?" he asked, because it wasn't like he could say the truth out loud.

She tucked her phone into her back pocket. "Because there are Swedish meatballs for you at the end of it, and then beer when we get back to Harbor City."

"Meatballs?" he asked, stepping out of the shower and following her out of the little fake bathroom.

"You've never had the IKEA meatballs?" She slipped her hand into the crook of his arm as they followed the arrows painted on the floor toward the next section of the showroom. "Oh, you are in for a treat."

His stomach growled, but he barely noticed anything beyond the brush of her hip against his. "How many more things are on the list?"

"Fifteen," she said with a sigh.

"You're doing the next one."

She looked down at the printed scavenger hunt list in her hand. "I can totally pretend to be asleep in a bed."

He almost tripped over his own feet as he imagined Chelle spread out on a bed, the sheets tangled up around her waist, and her amazing tits bare to the night air. Lust, sure and strong, sucker punched his dick and sucked all the air out of his lungs. Chelle shot him a questioning look as he tried his best to get his shit back together. Too bad that mental image of her was not leaving his head.

Yeah, good luck forgetting it—ever—Beckett.

Chapter Thirteen

CHELLE

Feet aching from walking a million miles in IKEA, Chelle settled back against the booth at Bottle Rocket and did her best not to notice the live wire of sexual awareness lighting her up from the inside.

The wine bar was down the block from Chelle's apartment, and she'd fallen in love with the place the moment she'd stepped inside the soft-lit cozy space. A hockey-themed wine bar may not be something that seemed to make sense at first, but Ice Knights player Alex Christensen was a guy that always made things happen on the ice and off of it. He was definitely a Harbor City favorite, which showed in the mix of clientele at the wine bar, where, in addition to the wine snobs, there were the Ice Knights fans and neighborhood regulars who showed up for the California rosé and conversation.

Chelle swore she always saw more folks from her building at Bottle Rocket than the quarterly tenant meetings. Of course, since the wine bar didn't include Chelle's building nemesis, Suzanne, who dreamed of being the tenant dictator, it was a lot more relaxing than tenant events—including the annual holiday party.

Which was next week and—to make it even more horrifying—her uncle would be there as Suzanne's date. Oh yeah, and there was no way Chelle could skip the event. Gut twisting in anticipated agony, she sank back against the tufted upholstery of the two-person booth at the back wall, closed her eyes, and let out a miserable groan.

"Should I have gotten an extra glass?" Nash asked.

Chelle cracked an eyelid open. "Probably an extra bottle."

He handed her a glass of pink-bubble goodness and sat down next to her, his thigh touching hers and sending a frisson of awareness shooting through her. "Anything I can help with?"

"Only if you can make my jerk of an uncle disappear permanently so I don't have to see him at the building holiday party." The words were out of her mouth before the alternate meaning of them was processed. "Wait. I didn't mean it that way."

Nash turned his head so his lips nearly brushed against her ear. "You mean you don't want me to off him?"

He wasn't serious, she knew that. Still, there was something a little feral in the way he said it that made her twisted little heart grow a few sizes. Okay, fine, it reminded her of the alpha heroes in her paranormal romances who went all in for their loves. Not that Nash loved her—or would ever love her—but mental muscle memory was a thing.

"Sweet of you to offer," she said, "but I look horrible in jailhouse orange."

He winked at her, setting off a whole heart-flutter thing, and took a drink of his wine. "I was concerned when the bartender said this was made with Concorde grapes, but it's actually really good."

"Yeah, it's my favorite," she said, taking a sip of the rosé, the tiny bubbles fizzing against her tongue before she swallowed. "It's happiness in a bottle, and who doesn't need a little of that?"

"You know, I could go to that holiday party with you," he said, double dimples on full display. "To run interference with your uncle. Really, it would seem a little weird if your husband didn't go."

"You'd do that?" Chelle tried to remember the last time she didn't have to go solo when a probable confrontation with family was involved and came up blank.

He shrugged. "Why not?"

"There will be games and mandatory fun with watered-down drinks," she said. "Why I ever suggested having a building holiday party, I have no idea."

Well, beyond the combined high of finishing a book and getting to dive into the annual reread of Ursula K. LeGuin's *The Earthsea Cycle*. Yep. Sometimes two rights did make a wrong, even if it didn't work the other way around.

"Maybe it will be so bad it will be good," Nash said.

"So it could be the ugly Christmas sweater of holiday parties?" She snorted, trying to imagine the perpetually uptight and bitchy Suzanne in a garish green-and-red sweater with a cat wearing a Santa hat on it. "It's going to be the absolute opposite of the perfect night, which would involve wine, a fireplace, and having my favorite book read to me. To think the party will be anything but misery, you must be an optimist."

"Some days." He took another drink of his wine as he glanced around at the Ice Knights memorabilia on the walls. "You know, we have a company suite at the Ice Knights arena. Maybe we can go sometime. Just not when they're playing the Cajun Rage. My cousin is a Rage fan, and he is unbearable during those games—even with Fiona shooting death glares at him that would make a normal man's balls explode."

"I take it she roots for the correct team?" Chelle asked with a chuckle.

Nash's blue eyes rounded comically. "Oh yeah, her family is pretty rabid—not to mention her brother-in-law is Zach Blackburn."

She lifted her wineglass in a toast. "To opposites attracting."

He tapped her glass with his, and after that they sat there, hip to hip, tucked into the narrow booth, and watched people in the bar as they flirted and gossiped and relaxed with friends. As a writer, observing folks was part of her daily existence. It made sense that someone whose job focused solely on how to get people to want things they didn't realize they needed in their lives would be as into people watching as she was. At that moment Nash nudged her and jerked his chin toward an older couple sharing a bottle in the corner, holding hands on the tiny table between them.

"Actually spies tracking down an international wine thief," he said.

Oh yeah, this was a game she could play.

"That guy in the gray plaid scarf is the number-one suspect," she said, looking in the direction of the guy with the floppy hair, sitting by himself at the end of the bar.

Nash stretched, and his arm came down across the back of the booth, casually curling around her shoulders and setting her pulse to ultra-aware mode. It was like being enveloped by a thick, knit blanket, soft and solid at the same time. And very, *very* warm.

"Of course," he said as he took another drink of his wine, "it could also be the woman over there in the head-to-toe black. She looks like she could kill a man with only her thumbs."

Chelle laughed out loud. She couldn't help it. He was right, the woman with a bunch of friends at one of the tables totally had the look of a well-trained assassin. "That's Ryder Falcon, and she probably *could* take someone out with only her thumbs. She and her brother Tony own this investigative firm I've used a few times."

She left off the part about using it to check him out before she agreed to get real married to a fake husband.

"Called it," Nash said and clinked her glass with his.

They spent the next few hours going back and forth between speculating on the secret life of the other people in the wine bar, stories about her pugs and his mom's chihuahua mix, and somewhat questionable wine puns (why have less scato when you can have mo' scato?) while finishing off the bottle of rosé they'd ended up getting. By the time Nash topped off her glass with the last of the wine, she was mellow, giggly, and more than a little horny. A woman could only spend so much time wrapped up in the almost-embrace of a sexy, thick rock of a man without worrying that her nipples had become perma-hard.

"You know," Nash said, pulling back so they weren't touching anymore, "we could renegotiate our agreement about nothing physical between us."

Did she really want that? The fizzy feeling bubbling inside her screamed *yes*. It took everything Chelle had not to scoot over to be touching him again.

"What are you thinking?" A quickie in the bathroom? Was she too old for that? Because at the moment, it seemed like a damn fine idea.

"That you're as attracted to me as I am to you," he said, absolutely 180 percent confident in his declaration.

Play it cool, Michelle. No, correction, play it cold.

Yeah, easier said than done when she was pretty much Mt. Vesuvius at the moment.

"That's a big assumption," she said, sounding more than a little breathy even to herself.

"But if it's true," he countered, "why not be adults about it and do what husbands and wives do?"

"Exchange icy glares and engage in passive-aggressive snit fits?" The question was out before she could censor herself.

Nash let out a low whistle. "Your parents' marriage must have been really something."

And this was why she didn't talk about her parents. They were, in a word, a nightmare. Still, she'd brought it up, so she might as well explain. "My dad had some very old-school, patriarchal views about a woman's place in a marriage, and my mom coped with pills and booze, which my dad pretended was a bug in their marriage as opposed to a feature." She forced a light tone into her voice despite the heavy ache in her chest. Old traumas always left scars. "I suppose your parents are married and living that perfect life?"

"Not even close," he said with a laugh that lacked his usual sincerity. "They're...well, they're a lot to take care of. I have to make sure the bills are paid, since neither of them will hire a business manager, then there's the reminding them of birthdays and important dates, and yeah, I have to check in but, despite it all, they are pretty amazing. My mom finds the good in almost every situation, and my dad, well, he's got a way of looking at the world that always makes me sit back and reevaluate what I'm doing. They're both smart, loving, and completely oblivious to all of the little things that have to be done to function in the real world."

Chelle pivoted in her seat, her hand dropping to his thigh. "Is that why you do what you do? All of the mansplaining and telling people what to do?"

"Someone has to, and I'm the oldest, so there it is." He drained the rest of the wine in his glass. "I make sure they don't Absentminded Professor their lives into a mess. They're good people. They're just preoccupied. A lot. You have brothers or sisters?"

She shook her head. "Only child."

"Do you talk to your mom still?"

"No, uh…she died when I was in high school."

He reached out and squeezed her hand. "I'm sorry."

Chelle mentally pressed back on all of the anxiety and hurt that started to swirl around in her chest. "Dad and I weren't close after I left the family fold, only the obligatory call on birthdays and holidays. If it wasn't for the family foundation, I'm not sure we would have talked beyond that." Realization of the emotional black hole they were walking toward hit her, and she pulled up before they crossed into the weepy stage of wine drinking. "Okay, we're supposed to be celebrating killing it at the IKEA scavenger hunt, not falling down the rabbit hole of how our parents messed us up."

Nash dropped his arm across the back of the booth again, his fingertips brushing against her shoulder. "Tell me about the foundation."

Chelle relaxed, and most of the sadness stirred to the surface by thoughts of her mom settled.

"It's small, but we have a solid crew of people who really care about helping people, and Hadley Donovan, our fundraising consultant, has made it possible for us to do that." Hiring Hadley after she'd just started her own business had been a risk, but wow, had it paid off. "We offer rental assistance, food subsidies, educational and training opportunities, and anything else we can possibly fund that can get real-world results for the folks that need it. I love making things better and helping people to flourish."

Outside of her books, the foundation was the only place where life guaranteed a happy ending—as long as she could stop her uncle Buckley from taking it over and shutting it down.

Nash lifted an eyebrow. "So you're helping without mansplaining?"

She chuckled. Okay, fine, he got her there. "Except people are actually asking for my help."

"I see." He glided his thumb over her shoulder, setting off a jumble of sensations through her. "And that's why you're helping me with the mansplaining and everything else?"

She let out a shaky breath. "You mean winning your bet?"

"I'd almost forgotten about the bet." Heat flared in his gaze when it dipped to her mouth as she took the last drink of her wine. "I guess I'm a little preoccupied with the possibility of us changing the rules of our marriage. Chelle...I want to seduce you. Would you be all right with that?"

A shiver of awareness zipped across her skin, she let out a shaky breath, and she barely managed to stop herself from answering with a *yes please* to his plan.

Instead, she did the smart, grown-ass woman thing and said, "I'll think about it."

As if she would be *not* thinking about it any time soon. The truth was she was having more and more difficulty not imagining Nash naked. Was there really any harm in a little no-strings fun with her husband?

Chapter Fourteen

CHELLE

It had been sixteen hours since Nash had told her that he wanted to seduce her, and she was still thinking about it. In fact, it was pretty much all she was thinking about.

Seriously. She was three self-induced orgasms—THREE!—into the day, and she was still coasting along that edge of I'm-gonna-go-fuck-my-fake-husband. It was so bad that she'd abandoned her book and was about to go take the dogs on their third walk of the day when she sniffed the unmistakable smell of fresh paint in the air.

It had to be in her head. Maybe she'd finally crossed that deadly line between reality and fiction her dad had always lectured her about when he caught her reading late into the night as a teen. She'd half convinced herself that the paint fumes were all in her head when she realized the dogs were sniffing the tiny sliver of space between her bedroom door and the floor.

No. Way.

She marched over to the door, flung it open, and the undeniable stench of semi-gloss slapped her across the face.

Yes. Way.

She found Nash in her tiny kitchen. The cabinets were taped off. The countertop was covered in plastic. The bistro table they'd eaten their cheeseburgers at the other day was tucked into a corner of the living room. Two wide stripes of paint covered a good-size swath of space above her kitchen sink. One was cornflower blue and the other was a gorgeous, mossy green that really fit with the dark, eclectic vibe of the rest of the apartment and made her fantasy book–loving soul give a happy sigh.

To be honest with herself, she wasn't sure if she was mad because she loved that color so much or because she hadn't had the ovaries to just paint the kitchen the shade she wanted. Who was going to know she'd done it? Also, it was a stupid clause in a dumb control-freak will and she owned the apartment now. It was hers to do what she wanted and—

She fisted her hands and let out a frustrated growl of a pissed-off groan.

Nash's shoulders drooped. "You hate it."

"Worse," she muttered. "I love it."

Nash shot her a double-dimple grin as he crossed over to her, pivoting so they stood next to each other, staring at the paint stripes on the wall. He didn't tower over her, not completely, but being this close to him was enough to scatter her thoughts in the direction of wondering what else he could do with those strong hands of his.

"I started talking to the graphic design team at Beckett Cosmetics as soon as I realized you wanted to change it."

What? "I never said that."

"Sure you did," he said as he crossed his thick arms over his chest. "You said you hated the color but that you yourself couldn't change it."

Something inside Chelle's chest shifted at the realization that he had listened to her. It wasn't that he nodded and added the uh-huhs at appropriate times like her dad had or offered meaningless platitudes like her mom had. He'd really listened and had given her words weight and value.

And that's when it clicked.

Nash wasn't seducing her by putting the moves on her. He was seducing her brain and appealing to her with acts of service at the same time.

Fucking A. *How am I supposed to resist that?*

"I, however, can paint it. Problem solved," he continued. "Now, the question is, blue or green? The graphic designers agreed both are soothing colors, and the green is the hot new shade for kitchens. The blue feels more traditionally kitchen, but the green makes me think of an enchanted forest. I don't know. It just sorta seems to fit the rest of your place with the sword and all."

Chelle would be lying to herself if she tried to act as if he wasn't right. He was. Her insides went all gooey at the realization that it was the exact shade she imaged the canopy of trees would be that Hermia walked under before her fateful first meeting with Bacchus in her books. She swallowed past the surprise of emotion that clogged her through at that and turned her head away from him so she could blink the sudden tears out of her eyes (damn pre-menopausal hormones).

She was just getting her shit back together when Nash's phone started buzzing. He picked it up off the plastic-covered countertop and grimaced at the screen.

"Your cousins?" she asked, because who else would it be?

"Yeah, they are having way too much fucking fun with this." He looked up and shot her a sheepish grin that only showed off one dimple. "You up for an underground tabletop board game club?"

Okay, that was not the date she expected. Did his cousins

not believe in dinner and a movie? "We're going to play Monopoly?"

"No." He shook his head. "We're gonna win Monopoly."

She couldn't help but laugh. This man. He really was nothing but trouble—which she needed to remember, because nothing about this situation was real, even if standing in her paint-prepped kitchen felt like it.

"So what about the kitchen color?" he asked. "Do you want me to change it back to yellow?"

Chelle's first instinct was to push back against the change just for the sake of proving that she could. However, the truth of it was that she hated the yellow—and, no, hate wasn't too heavy of a word for how she felt. It really was eye-searing.

She gave in with a happy sigh. "I love the green."

He brushed a kiss across her temple, which sent a lightning bolt of awareness through her.

"You won't regret this," he said as he started back toward the paint cans.

Yeah, *he* was sure of that, but as she snuck a peek at Nash's muscular forearms as he pulled up the sleeves of his already paint-splattered Henley, it sent her thoughts right back to Midlife Crisis Younger Husband Horny Town, and *she* wasn't so sure about that.

Chapter Fifteen

Nash

"I can't believe you got us kicked out of a tabletop board game club before we even sat down." Chelle was laughing so hard she could barely get the words out. "What were you thinking?"

All around their seats at the counter in Vito's Diner was complete chaos, with the jukebox blaring out old songs from the eighties, people packed into booths to grab a bite before the shows started in the theater district, and a line of hungry customers that went out the door and down the block. However, Nash couldn't tear his attention away from Chelle as she continued to teasingly give him shit about the disaster that was their second date.

"I was thinking that the guy running the check-in process was completely overwhelmed and starting to drown in flop sweat," Nash said in his halfhearted defense, because he wasn't so much interested in proving he was right as keeping Chelle talking. "He needed some insight."

"So you thought telling him how to do his job—" She held up a finger in the universal sign of *hold on one minute* as she sucked in a breath between giggles. "No, correction, you thought telling him how to do the thing he volunteers his time for would be a good idea?"

He got it. He'd done the thing again, but the last thing Nash wanted was for the guy in head-to-toe Master of the Games wizarding cosplay to have a bunch of people mad at him because it was taking so long to find people's registrations.

"What?" Nash snagged one of the few fries left on Chelle's plate and popped it into his mouth. "You wanted me to sit there and let the poor guy suffer?"

Chelle wiped away her tears of amusement as she got her giggle fit under control. "Or—walk with me on this one— you could have simply asked him if he needed help and then helped according to what he said he needed rather than what you think he needs instead of offering up a ten-minute lecture the poor guy definitely didn't want while the line got longer and longer behind us."

Nash stuffed his natural defensive response down and thought about it for a minute. The guy had been sweaty, but he'd also just rushed into the room and let everyone know that the printer was being an asshole. That meant he had to go by handwritten notes instead of the spreadsheet from the Google form and—

Fuck.

That guy had his shit together. He'd just needed some time to get his bearings together.

Way to go, Beckett. Open mouth, insert foot.

"You might be right," he said, stealing another fry from Chelle's plate to soften the blow to his ego.

Chelle turned her stool so she faced him completely and then raised an eyebrow. "Might be?"

He stalled her from saying anything else that he'd have

to admit she was right about by swiping a third fry from her plate. This time, however, he dragged it through the ketchup and offered it up as a peace offering. "Truce?"

"Only because you know I'm right," she said as she took the fry and popped it into her mouth.

His fingers were still tingling from the brush of her fingers when their waitress, Carlene, showed up on the other side of the counter where they were sitting. Her dangling hamburger earrings were swinging with the force she used to chomp her gum, and her order pad was at the ready, but otherwise she seemed impervious to the other diners trying to get her attention.

"You two lovebirds want dessert or the check?" she asked between snaps of her gum.

"It seems a little busy tonight," Nash said.

"Yeah," Carlene scoffed. "Denise called in sick, and Ruby is not long for the waitressing world."

They glanced over at the only other waitress in the place. The woman who looked like a stiff harbor breeze would send her flying down First Avenue was carrying a tray overloaded with milkshakes. She weaved a little to the left, then a little toward the right in her efforts to keep the heavy tray right side up, until she got to a table of six tourists and set it down with a relieved sigh.

"You know," he said, turning back to face Carlene, "one option may be if you divided up—"

Chelle reached over and gave an unmistakable stop-before-our-waitress-stabs-you-with-a-kitchen-knife squeeze to his knee. It was just enough to send his thoughts in two directions faster than Christensen with a breakaway puck at an Ice Knights game. One, Nash really wanted Chelle's hand to keep going northward. Two, he could actually be the one to take advice every once in a while, and maybe this was one of those times.

"Let me try that again." He gave their waitress his most charming smile. "Would you like some free help tonight?"

Carlene looked from him to Chelle and back again. "Do you have any experience?"

He shook his head. "None."

"Too bad, we don't train amateurs here. If you wanna help, leave a big tip," Carlene said, putting her pen to her order pad again. "Now, do you want dessert or the check? There's people waiting for your stools."

It was like losing out on a bet with his cousins. First there was the shock of it even happening at all, and then there was the annoyance at himself for not doing better, for not doing what it took to make sure everyone had what they needed.

"Dessert, please," Chelle said, filling in the empty space when he should have answered. "Apple pie, two forks, and an Oreo shake, two straws."

"You got it." Carlene dashed off a notation on the order pad and then she was gone, making her way down the counter to the next couple who had been waiting to place their order.

Her hand still resting on his knee, Chelle asked, "If I promise that you can have the cherry that comes on top of the shake, will that ease your pain?"

Right now, he wasn't so much concerned with pain as the way every nerve in his dick was tuned in to her hand. It wasn't that having his offer of help turned down didn't still sting, but one of the hottest women in the world, who also happened to be married to him—if only temporarily—was literally inches from touching his cock. He was going through some things, okay?

Still, sitting here silent wasn't really going to do anything to persuade Chelle that he wasn't a complete fool, so he managed to string together some words. "I really could have helped."

"But you're gonna leave a good tip, right?"

He wasn't a complete dipshit. "Yeah."

"Well," Chelle said with a smile, "I'll cover the check, and you leave a ginormous tip, and that will give her the help she actually wants, not the kind you think she needs." Her hand traveled up his thigh an inch before she seemed to realize what she was doing and pulled back, flexing her fingers as her cheeks turned bright red. "Deal?"

How the fuck was he supposed to argue with her logic when it was right on target? "You're kind of obnoxious when you're right."

"Are you going to hold that against me in the divorce?"

Fuck. That little bit of reality was like a sucker punch to the kidneys, but he managed not to flinch. "Absolutely."

"Fair enough." She pivoted back in her stool so she faced the counter, moving her glass of water and nearly empty plate to the side so Carlene, who was making her way back over to them, would have room to set down the pie and shake. "I'm holding the fact that you moved my coffee table to the perfect spot and picked out my new favorite color for the kitchen against you when I talk to the judge."

Carlene put the shake and the apple pie with a ginormous scoop of vanilla ice cream between them and then slapped the check down on the counter before moving on to take care of another customer.

"Sounds like it's going to be a contentious divorce," he said as he grabbed the cherry from the top of the shake's mountain of whipped cream and ate it. "Don't worry, it'll be worth it."

Chapter Sixteen

NASH

What first caught Nash's attention two hours after he and Chelle came home from their date and went to their separate bedrooms was her dogs' determined scratches at his closed bedroom door. And when he opened his door, he heard it.

At first, he wasn't sure. Maybe? Nah, his dick had to be influencing his ears. Then again, that was a pretty unique sound.

She'd said she'd think about it.

Was she thinking about it with battery-powered help?

Still half asleep but waking up as fast as his dick was hardening, he peeked out into the dark hallway toward Chelle's bedroom. A narrow strip of light escaped the pug-sized opening between her door and the frame. Holding his breath, he listened to the steady buzzing and tried to convince himself that she was brushing her teeth with an electric toothbrush. That's all the buzzing was. Dental hygiene was important, and maybe she'd woken up and realized she'd forgotten to brush after their night out.

Then a quiet, needy moan came from her room, and that theory went straight to hell.

Chelle was getting off with a vibrator.

Fuck.

He gripped his doorframe, white knuckling the shit out of that wood rather than his own, because jaysus f'ing christ the mental images flying through his head were basically life-altering.

Her long fingers, nails painted cherry red, wrapped around a shiny silver vibe slipping between her thick thighs.

The arch of her back when she hit that spot—the one that turned her on so much she didn't even realize her pugs had pulled a Houdini.

The way her lips would part as her breath sped up, then she'd use the tip of her tongue to wet her bottom lip before biting down on it in an effort not to make any noise.

But it would be hard, so fucking hard, because the metal had warmed to the overheated temperature of her wet slit.

Then, she'd slide it inside, lift her hips to meet her thrusts, fuck herself for a while, cupping her tits, rolling her nipples, her eyes closed, her dark hair slipping free of the messy bun she'd had it pulled up in for the night, and just when she thought she couldn't take it anymore, she'd dial up the intensity pulses and pull it out. She'd drag it around her swollen clit, dip it back inside, and keep that on repeat, getting herself so close to coming again and again that her nipples would be red and tender from her twisting them as she rode that almost-but-not-quite wave.

And that's why, according to his very vivid fantasy, she'd lost her control enough for that moan to escape.

But what was she picturing while she played with herself?

Lust, flame hot and as tangible as a fist to the face, blasted through him, knocking the last vestiges of sleep out of his brain. Hell, he might never sleep again, and he was more than okay with that.

There were so many possibilities.

Was it a faceless lover, there to do exactly what she wanted the second she told him?

Was it a group? Male? Female? Nonbinary? All of the above?

Was it a stranger? Someone she knew? *Him?* His head between her legs, inhaling the sweet scent of her pussy as she ground her clit against his mouth, her fingers gripping his hair and holding him in place until she got exactly what she wanted?

Would she be quiet, only moans and panting? Would she have a dirty mouth that detailed all of the things she wanted him to do, all of the things she'd do to him? Would she yell out as she came, her plushy thighs tightening against the sides of his head as he tongued her to another orgasm and another after that until she was limp with pleasure?

His hand was around his rock-hard dick tenting his sweatpants before he even realized it.

Breathing hard, he barely managed to stop himself from stroking his cock to the sound of Chelle getting off.

He needed to turn around, go back in his room, and close the door. Then he'd get in bed, close his eyes, and stare at the back of his eyelids for the better part of eternity until dawn came. That's what he should do, right? It seemed like it, but instead, here he was still standing here holding onto the doorframe above his head like it would anchor him to the spot and keep him from stalking down the hallway to her room. He hadn't been invited. She probably didn't even realize he could hear her. If the dogs hadn't done the whole escape artist thing, he doubted he would have woken up and realized what was going on.

So get back in your room, asshole.

He would if he could, but he couldn't get his body to listen to what he knew was the right thing.

He had no idea how it could get worse, then he heard her sharp inhale a second before she let out a groan that had the tip of his dick slick and his balls tightening up.

Teeth clamped tight and his grip on the doorframe hard enough to leave finger dents, he was still trying to catch his breath and not come in his pants a few seconds, minutes, years later when Chelle let out a satisfied moan and the buzzing stopped. Nash was still being flooded with images of what her O face was like when she muttered "shit" and her door opened the rest of the way.

He froze in his open doorway.

The low light from her room put a soft glow around her as she stood there in a white sleep shirt decorated with a woman sitting on a massive stack of books under the words "so many books, so little time." It stopped about mid-thigh and had a loose, low-scooped neck that showed off the tops of her pillowy tits. It had a faded stain near the hip that looked like it had survived through many washes. Her hair had gone wild and she had that soft, relaxed look of someone who'd just blasted their body with orgasmic happy hormones.

She was—without a doubt—the sexiest thing he'd ever seen.

"Mary Puppins! Groucho Barks!" she whisper-yelled as she tucked her loose hair behind her ears. "Get back here right now."

That's when she spotted him.

The whole world stopped on its axis in the time between one heartbeat and the next.

Whatever the woman did for fun, it should not be playing poker, because in that timeframe the expressions on her face went from shock to confusion to embarrassment that turned her cheeks pink to an annoyance that had him harder than that vibe she'd been using.

"Were you"—she let out a little squeak of embarrassment—"*listening* to me?"

Yep. Creep-O-Meter 2000 alert. "I didn't mean to."

"Really?" She wrapped her arms around her middle.

Fuck. This was why he should have gone back in his room and pretended he'd never heard anything.

"The dogs," he said, stumbling over those two little words as the animals in question sprinted out of his room and back into Chelle's. "They scratched at my door and then I heard—"

Her cheeks flushed an even brighter shade of pink. "The buzzing?"

He nodded. "Yeah."

"How long did you listen?"

"Long enough." Or not enough, or too long. Hell, he had no idea how to answer that one.

"Good night, Nash." She started to turn but then stopped halfway and bit down on her bottom lip.

His pulse went to jackhammer speed, and all the air whooshed out of his lungs as he waited for whatever was coming next.

She peeked over at him, a nervous smile playing at her lips. "I suppose there's only one way to make things even."

Of all the things she could have said, he'd never even considered that. Still, his cock fucking ached at the possibilities as he tried—and failed—to come up with some kind of response.

"My idea is simple," she went on, her voice so quiet he wasn't sure for a minute that she was talking to him. "You keep one arm up like it is on the doorframe. Use the other to jerk yourself off in your sweats. You do not get to take your dick out." Her gaze darted up to his face and then back down to the floor before she turned the rest of the way around. "I'll just listen. We'll never talk of it again. But only if you agree.

No pressure, Nash. Go back in your room and close the door, and we'll act like this never happened at all. I mean it."

He had absolutely no doubt of her sincerity or her nerves. She was giving him an out—and an opportunity. He didn't have to think twice about which one he was going to take.

"Chelle."

She stilled immediately. "That's a no, then." She mumbled something to herself that sounded a lot like "what did you expect, Michelle" and looked over her shoulder at him, her gaze landing everywhere but on him. "No worries. I shouldn't have—"

"That was absolutely *not* a no, Chelle." He loosened the string at his waist and shoved his hand down, gripping his cock like a man holding on for dear fucking life.

Heat blazed in her eyes as she watched him for the count of five before turning back around and saying in a voice more high-pitched and shaky than usual, "You have to stroke it."

As if he didn't already know that.

"I know how to get myself off," he said as he shuffled his hand up and down his dick, slicking the wetness on the head down the shaft in the process, one more sign that he was not going to last long.

"Kind of annoying when someone tells you your own business, huh?" she teased, as if trying to take some of the tension out of the situation.

Of course, that wasn't going to happen. He liked the tension. Wanted it. Craved it.

"Is that what this is?" he managed to get out while he fucked his hand and stared at the way her round ass pushed against her sleep shirt. "A lesson?"

She shook her head, making her hair move over her shoulders, and he had a vision of roping the long, dark strands around his hand as he fucked her from behind, in front of a mirror. He could see the way her ass would bounce and how her tits would shake and the sweet sight of her mouth half open as she told him to fuck her harder.

He nearly came right then but caught himself just in time, wanting to extend the pleasure of this.

"It's not a lesson, Nash," Chelle said. "It's positive reinforcement. Associating something that feels very, very good with new behavior—in your case, listening to someone else."

The way she said his name, something in the breathy tone of her voice, sent his hand into overdrive as his balls tightened. His breath was coming in ragged pants as he got closer and closer.

"That's it, Nash, hard and fast and needy," she went on, her voice sounding ragged as if she was almost as close to the edge of coming as he was, even though she wasn't touching herself. "I bet you'd love to sink that big cock of yours right inside me. Is that what you were thinking about while you were listening to me masturbate? Fucking me? Railing me? Blowing out my back and leaving me dick drunk and worn out?"

"No." God, he was so close, and the way she was talking had him a hairsbreadth away from losing it. "I was imagining what you look like when you play with yourself, who you wanted to touch you, how you'd want them to do it, and what it would be like to have you come all over my mouth so many times you couldn't think anymore."

And that's all it took, that mental image of her sweaty, satisfied, and slick, to send him right over the edge, coming hard enough in his sweats that he lost the ability to see anything at all.

Blood rushed freight-train loud in his ears as he sucked air into his lungs, as if he'd been drowning—which in a way, he kinda had been. He'd been drowning in Chelle Finch without ever touching her, and it was a helluva amazing way to go.

"Good night, Nash," Chelle said.

By the time he had it together enough to open his eyes and focus on her bedroom door, it was already closed. He watched until the line of light escaping from underneath it went out.

Fuck me.

He'd fucked models, heiresses, and even a pair of best friends who had a thing for double blow jobs in dark restaurants. He'd jerked off a million times since he got his first hard-on after watching Amelia Hunter stretch before gym class. He was a member of the private jet mile-high club, sexted like a pro, and had blown off steam more than once with a fuck buddy who loved no-strings dick appointments that occasionally involved pegging him just right.

Still, jerking off in Chelle's hallway while she didn't watch him was without a doubt the hottest thing he'd ever experienced.

They were definitely going to talk about this again.

Tomorrow morning.

There was no way she wouldn't bring it up.

He couldn't wait.

Chapter Seventeen

CHELLE

The next morning, Chelle had almost convinced herself that she could totally hide in her room for the rest of her life. Who would blame her? She hadn't been herself last night. She'd been...someone totally else. It was like she'd had a super horny, kinda-but-not-really kinky out-of-body experience and had been so turned on by the idea of Nash hearing her get off that she'd gone all bossy on him and told him how to jerk off.

Even worse, she wanted to do it again.

Well, not exactly that. She wanted to do more. So much more. Like all of the more.

How in the hell was she supposed to keep that bit of truth off her face when she walked out of her bedroom? As Karmel always said, Chelle's face wasn't just an easy read, it was like an audiobook that someone had turned up all the way, then broke the volume button and thrown it into the harbor.

The dogs whined at her bedroom door, the one she'd

quadruple checked was closed, and gave her the doggie equivalent of the gotta-go-right-now dance.

That was it!

Dog walking took precedence over talking. Right? Right. After that?

She'd figure it out. She always did. A woman didn't hit her forties without getting a master's degree in personal disaster management.

Keeping her head down, she hustled out of her room and headed straight for the dog leashes hanging from a hook by the front door, Mary and Groucho happy yapping at her ankles the whole way. That's when Sir Hiss meowed from the kitchen, drawing her attention and completely blowing her perfect(ish) plan.

Nash stood in the archway dividing her tiny kitchen from the foyer, a skillet in one hand and spatula in the other. Instead of last night's gray sweatpants hanging low on his hips, he was wearing a pair of jeans that highlighted the mouth-watering power of his rock-hard thighs and a navy Henley that made his eyes seem even more blue. The sleeves of his shirt were pushed up and showed off just enough forearm to make her mouth go dry.

"Going somewhere?" he asked without any of the heat making his gaze spark.

Words. She needed to make words. Make words? How about use words?

Holy cow, and you call yourself an author?

Yes, she did. Writing and speaking with the guy who'd tapped into some sexy boss part of herself she didn't even know she had were not the same thing. One made sense. The other was about as logical as the marriage requirement in her dad's will. That little reminder brought her brain back to the reality of the situation—she had a fake husband for a very limited time of one month so that she could stop her asshole uncle from closing the Finch Foundation.

That was all.

There was nothing else here—no matter what the squadron of rogue butterflies in her stomach were saying.

"I'm taking the dogs for their morning walk," she said as she clipped Mary's leash to her collar.

"I'll join you." He sat the pan down on the stovetop and turned off the burner.

Groucho's leash slipped in her hand at the proposal. Nash? Going on a dog walk? After last night? The idea made her palms sweaty, and she sucked in a calming breath before saying, "I'm not sure that's a good idea. They have a routine."

"Can I come with you? Please?" he asked, then looked at her, a smile starting to curl the corners of his mouth upward. "Positive reinforcement and all that."

She opened her mouth to tell him no, but nothing came out because he was looking at her like the puppy she'd teased him about being. He was all pleading eyes and sweet energy. Then he gave her the full double-dimple grin, and her resistance wilted like a bouquet of magical pansies from her books when they got hit with the harsh light of a sorcerer's wand in mid-spell.

"All right." Giving in to the inevitable, she held out the handle of Mary's leash with a weary sigh that there was no way he was going to buy as legit. "Let's go."

They made it down the stairs in silence—that was if no one counted the dogs' happy yaps that echoed just enough in the stairwell that Chelle knew she'd be getting a nastygram from Suzanne about her dogs disturbing the building's residents (AKA Suzanne). After they cleared the lobby door, they got hit by a blast of feels-like-winter-even-if-it-wasn't-officially-December-twenty-third wind that blasted the chitchat right out of her.

A few minutes later, they were half a block away from her

building, and Nash hadn't said a single word yet, either. Aside from a few sidelong glances that sent a shiver through her, which had nothing to do with the chill in the air, he was quiet. No unsolicited advice about the correct amount of slack to have in the leash. No out-of-the-blue tidbits about the best route to take to give Mary and Groucho the optimum step-to-sniff ratio. No unasked-for opinions about the type of poop bags she had, the proper length of each break so the dogs could sniff the fire hydrants, or the ideal amount of space to leave between the pugs and any oncoming pooches.

There was no way one observed orgasm was responsible for all that. Nash was holding back. Why?

It was nice, though, the companionable silence as they made the U-turn at the corner of Forty-Fifth and headed back toward her building, stopping every few steps for Groucho to mark a mailbox, bike rack, or the ginormous planters filled this time of year with poinsettias she always had to keep Mary from taking a bite of.

Ideally, all of this silence would give her plenty of time to think about something—anything—to talk about except what they'd done last night. Of course, that meant all she could think about was how wet she'd gotten when she'd heard him come. Just thinking about it had her breathing harder than necessary.

By the time they were back in the lobby and heading up the stairs to her apartment, the anticipation was killing her. Was he going to say anything about last night? It had happened. It hadn't been a case of her imagination running away during a solo sex session fantasy.

Fine, she'd been the one to say that they wouldn't talk about it again, but what kind of person would take her seriously about that? What kind of person could just pretend it had never happened?

Once inside her apartment, she unclipped and hung up

Groucho's leash while he did the same for Mary Puppins.
Then they just sort of stood there in the entryway, staring at
each other. She had no idea when this had started to become
a game of who can be quiet the longest, but it seemed like
it had gone that way. This was not who she was. She was a
chatter, a talker, a woman who liked to tell a story or twelve.
She was about to burst with all of the words building up inside
her, when he broke the silence.

"Okay, really, what are you getting up to in your room?"
he asked as his gaze dipped down to her mouth.

The look in his eyes was intense enough to sear her skin
and suck the jumble of words out of her head with an audible
whoosh. Good Lord. This was what it was like to feel naked
while fully dressed.

"During the day, I mean," he said after a deliberate
pause. "I've heard you during the past few days typing away,
and sometimes you talk to yourself in different voices."

No, she most definitely did not talk to herself. She cringed
and screwed up her face as about a billion examples of how
she'd gone over her main characters talking to each other
and, to be honest, acted out their interactions filled her head.
Fine, she did. She totally did talk to herself, but that was her
writing process, and she refused to be embarrassed about it—
no matter what lies the heat beating her cheeks told.

Really, there was no harm in telling him what only
Karmel knew. It wasn't so much that she was keeping it a
secret as that she didn't have anyone else to share it with. Did
that make her sound like she had one friend and pretty much
no one else? Yeah, well, reality was like that sometimes.

"I'm writing a book," she said as she walked into the
kitchen.

"Oh, that's cool," he said, following her into the tiny
galley. "What's it about?"

Chelle grabbed the two dog bowls from their spot on

a shelf above the sink and scooped dry food from a cookie canister on the counter. "It's part of a fantasy series."

While she supervised the dogs eating—Groucho was true to his namesake, kind of a dick when it came to protecting his food—Nash reached into the fridge and grabbed the carton of eggs he'd bought the other day. He set to work cracking eggs, pouring in some heavy cream, and adding a few seasonings that hadn't been in her cabinet before, then beating the mixture like it had insulted his mother. Finally, he poured them into the pan where he'd been sautéing some spinach and chopped tomatoes.

She wasn't sure whether she was watching because it all smelled so good and she hadn't had breakfast yet, or because Nash looked fucking hot in the kitchen with a daisy dishtowel slung over one shoulder. There was also the fact that he'd started a playlist and was dancing while he chopped, stirred, and tilted the cast-iron pan so that the egg mixture covered the veggies. His butt looked good when he did a little shake-shake thing.

Mouth-watering? Hers? Yeah, for the food, definitely for the food.

She turned around before she made a fool of herself by drooling and grabbed the box of Fruit Loops from the top of the fridge. Nash's *tsk-tsk* sound stopped her before she opened a cabinet to get a bowl.

"What?" she asked.

He gestured toward the pan with the clementine he was peeling. "I'm making you breakfast."

"You don't have to do that." But it was sweet, and part of her kinda liked the idea of having someone want to help her, instead of expecting her to always be the one helping simply because of her gender and her family's dedication to outdated patriarchal bullshit.

"I know I don't, but I'm doing it anyway. You know,

breakfast is the most important meal of the day." He folded his arms across his chest, laughter glimmering in his eyes as if he knew he was pushing her buttons. "Skipping breakfast is associated with an increased risk of diabetes and heart disease."

"I have these." Chelle shook the cereal box. "I don't need you mansplaining the importance of breakfast to me."

"How about you let me take care of you instead?" He cut a piece of the frittata and slid it onto a plate, garnishing it with a few sprigs of parsley and adding clementine slices to the plate. "Think of it as a thank-you for helping me win the bet with my cousins."

The bet? Her gut dropped and she managed—just barely—not to flinch back. In the past week, she'd forgotten all about Nash's reasons for their limited-time-only marriage. He didn't want to be married any more than she did, which was what made the arrangement so perfect. Now, the question was would she be able to make it three more weeks without spending way too much time thinking about what he was packing in those gray sweatpants?

Probably not.

Chelle took the plate with a thank-you and sat down at the barely big enough for two plates bistro table at the end of the kitchen, underneath the window that led out to the fire escape. Nash joined her with his matching breakfast. His oversize-lumberjack-of-a-man frame shouldn't look comfortable at the itty-bitty table, and yet he fit right in. Some people were like that. Nash Beckett was obviously one of them.

He lasted three bites before he set his fork down on his plate and looked her straight in the eyes. "Are you going to let me read your book?"

"No," she said without hesitation, while stuffing down her panic at the idea of anyone—*anyone*—reading her work. "I'm working on book four. No one wants to start on book four."

Nash's eyes went wide. "You have three books already done?"

That nervous buzzing that always made her feel all jittery partnered with that roller coaster boosted with nitro feeling in the stomach she always got when she talked about her books had her putting her fork down. The frittata was good. Not puking it up because she was peeling back a layer of her skin and cutting open a vein of vulnerability was better.

"You gotta let me read them."

He propped his forearms on the table, which meant his fingers were within millimeters of hers, which meant she added the warm, needy tease of desire to the buzzing and the stomach flopping. She was about half a second from adding super-sexy palm sweating to the mix when both of his dimples made an appearance.

Oh God, she was about to get the full court Nash Beckett charm offensive.

"I could give you free feedback," he said with all the confidence of a guy who manspread on a crowded train.

Okay, she was getting what Nash thought of as a charm offensive. It took a lot of control not to laugh out loud at his idea.

"That sounds like the absolute worst version of hell." Oops. Okay, that may have been too harsh—if 100 percent the truth.

If he was offended, he didn't show it as he asked, "Me reading them or me giving my thoughts?"

"Both," she said after a few seconds of thought. "Definitely both."

"Who has read them?"

She shrank back her chair. "Me."

He nodded and waved his hand in the air as if to urge her on. "And?"

She shot him her best shut-up glare—fine, it wasn't the greatest one, but she was still working her way up to it. Still, it didn't have any impact at all.

"Are you serious?" His you've-got-to-be-kidding-me laugh filled the room and got the dogs all excited and yappy. "Please, let me read them." He took her hands in his and brushed his thumb across the tops of her knuckles. "I won't say anything about them. No advice. No feedback. No critique. Nothing. I just want to read them."

Maybe it was because his touch scattered her sense of self-preservation to the wind, but she believed him. He hadn't said a single word about last night and he'd had every opportunity. Hell, she was ready to break her own rule banning talking about last night when he started making her breakfast. If he stuck to his word about that, then he could stick to it when it came to her book, right? She could just pretend he wasn't reading it.

"No talking?" she asked, a jittery sense of excitement mixed with dread making her skin prickly.

He gave her hands a reassuring squeeze. "Not a single word."

Oh God, she was going to regret this.

"Fine." She slipped her hands free of his, picked up her phone from the table, and AirDropped the file of her first book to Nash's phone. "But I'm holding you to your word. We never mention this book again."

"Yes, ma'am," he said as he stood up and gathered the dishes before carrying them to the sink where he started the water.

Shock at having someone help with a domestic chore had her glued to her chair with her mouth open for a second before she came to her senses. "I can do that."

"I don't mind." Nash snagged the dishcloth hanging from the oven handle and handed it to her. "How about I wash and you dry? You know where all the dishes go anyway. It'll be relaxing."

"Dishes are relaxing?" Yeah, that word didn't mean what he seemed to think it meant.

"Yeah." He flashed a grin at her, but unlike the usual one—or even the double dimpler—it didn't reach his eyes. "You clean it up and everything stays how it is supposed to be, then you can relax."

He cut off whatever she may have asked after that by turning up his playlist and dancing in front of the sink as he scrubbed the dishes clean.

She was drying a plate at that moment when the realization hit that there just might be more to Nash than a mansplainer so committed to winning a bet that he was willing to get married to a stranger to win it.

And that meant nothing but trouble for her.

Chapter Eighteen

CHELLE

"You did what?" Karmel asked, wide eyed, with her chocolate hazelnut croissant stopped halfway to her mouth.

She'd said it loud enough to get some stares from the folks sitting at tables around theirs at Grounded Coffee, who'd already spotted the woman from that one show (it was a different one for everyone) but were ignoring Karmel the way only jaded Harbor Citians could.

Chelle waited a few beats for the gawkers to turn back to their own tables and lowered her voice. "I listened to him jerk off."

Now Karmel was grinning, a devious little upturn of her mouth that showed just how much she was about to enjoy whatever came next. Chelle braced herself. She knew this would happen when she walked into the coffee shop no matter how much she mentally warned herself to just keep her mouth shut about Nash. Karmel had a way of just pulling the truth out of her—whether it was the reality of what growing up a rich Finch had been like or what she'd been up to with her (Karmel's words) hot hunk of a husband.

"And he did this," Karmel continued after taking a bite of chocolatey, flaky deliciousness, "because you told him to?"

Chelle sank lower in her chair and mumbled an affirmative into her toasted almond latte with extra foam.

"What was that? I couldn't hear you."

Okay, big girl, grown-ass woman panties time. Chelle sat up straighter and forced herself to make eye contact with her too-amused-to-hide-it friend. "Yes."

"Michelle Finch, you dirty bird," Karmel said with her signature husky laugh that grabbed the attention of a few more coffee shop patrons, who then glanced away almost as quickly as they started staring. "I'm impressed."

Yeah. That was one way to look at it. Guilt stole all of the taste from her latte as she took another drink. "With what, that I sexually harassed my fake husband?"

"Is that what it was?" Karmel added enough sugar packets to her plain black coffee to qualify it as a dessert. "Did he not listen to you first?" She sipped from her mug, wrinkled her nose, and then added a strong pour of liquid creamer. "Did you intimidate, use force, or otherwise coerce him into masturbating while your back was turned? Is there a power dynamic I'm not aware of?"

It wasn't that simple. "Not exactly, but—"

Karmel rolled her eyes and shook her head. "You two need to have a conversation." Then she lowered her theater-trained voice meant to reach the old lady in the back row with her hearing aid turned off to as close of a whisper as the woman had. "And you need to fuck him already, because where there are sizzling solo hand jobs there is also fire fucking."

"That's not a good idea," Chelle said before her mutinous libido could start rationalizing exactly how and why it was a very, very good idea.

"Fuck good ideas," Karmel said. "It's about time you had a little fun."

Fun? That really wasn't part of her make-up any more than relationships were. Fun belonged on the pages of her fantasy books, the short side quests that involved drunk goblins with the giggles and retrieving gemstones infused with aphrodisiac spells.

"He's too young," she said.

Karmel dead-eyed her. "There's barely a blip of an age difference between you. It's what, less than a decade?"

"Eight years." She was out of college when he'd been a high school freshman. He was a baby, a puppy, a—

Full-grown man packing a dick big enough to make her mouth water, going by what she'd seen when she'd looked at his gray sweatpants last night.

Shut up, brain.

"Uh-huh." Her friend shot her a that's-what-I-thought look over her mug of what in no way resembled anything close to coffee anymore.

"It's not like we're even *together* together." They were, after all, only husband and wife on paper, and they had agreed to no sexy times—even if he had suggested tearing up that part of the agreement.

Karmel gave her a so-what eyebrow raise.

"He'd probably mansplain the female orgasm to me." Why did that kinda sound hot? Oh God. She needed help. Professional help.

"I don't know about that." Karmel smirked. "Sounds to me like he's open to taking orders."

"I caught him off guard, and anyway, that's not really my thing."

Karmel scoffed. "Keep telling yourself that. You've spent your whole life having other people tell you what you want and how you should want it and what you should do to get it, but all of that 'touch yourself' stuff came out of nowhere?"

Vibrator-assisted fantasies and the joy of controlling all sorts of characters in her books aside? "It was a one-time occurrence."

"Sounds to me like you both need to figure out if that's really the case." Karmel sat her mug down. "You know I love you."

Chelle took a drink of her latte and braced herself for whatever was coming next, because she highly doubted she was going to want to hear it.

"But," her friend continued, "maybe it's time you get out of your own head and enjoy life rather than just watching it from the sidelines."

"I don't do that. I have a very full life with a job I love, hobbies, and my pets."

"And no one to share it with."

"That's perfectly fine with me." It gave her all the time in the world to do what she wanted, when she wanted, and how she wanted. It was freeing. "The last thing I need in my life is a man who thinks he can tell me what to do."

"Then you should be the one telling him what to do," Karmel said. "Nash isn't going to be in your life forever? Good, then this could be your chance to baby step it into the world of relationships. Try it on for size. Get your feet wet. Take it for a test drive. And if you get nothing but orgasms out of it, where is the harm in that? Like I told you before, life is a buffet and it's time for you to get fat and sassy on the bounty. Honey, you deserve it."

Why did all of that have to make so much sense, and what could Chelle even say to that? If she was writing one of her characters, she'd have plenty to say, but as herself? Yeah, it sounded a little too real.

Karmel reached across the table, covered Chelle's hand

with her own, and gave it a squeeze. "Just say you'll think about it."

As if she had been thinking of anything else over the past twenty-four hours. "Fine, I'll give it some thought."

"Some dirty thoughts, I hope," her friend said with a theatrically lewd wink.

Despite everything, Chelle burst out laughing. "You're a bad influence."

"Proudly and always." Karmel popped the last bite of her croissant into her mouth. "And you love me for it."

Now that, Chelle didn't have to think about at all, because it was 100 percent true. And as for what to do moving forward with Nash? She already knew the answer to that, she just wasn't sure she was ready to say it out loud.

Chapter Nineteen

Nash hadn't been so nervous for a date in his entire life.

Literally.

He'd spent the past few days inhaling Chelle's first book in between work meetings. He was so caught up in an epic battle between warring satyr families and wondering if his phone would melt from the fuck-ton of sex everyone was having that he'd missed his initial third-date reminder ping, and his second, and his third. By the time he'd gotten in his much needed ice-cold shower, he was already running late. Then, faced with the decision of what to wear out on his third date with the woman who'd managed to get him to read his first book in years that didn't have the phrase "steps to success," "quantitative growth," or "good to great" somewhere in the first chapter, he'd lost his nerve.

And that's why he'd called in his sister.

"Thank God you FaceTimed me because there is no way you can wear *that* sweater on a food truck crawl," Bristol said, wrinkling her nose in disgust.

He looked at himself in the mirror. Okay, the cuffs on his cream-colored sweater were a little frayed, but it was December. "Why not?"

His sister lifted an eyebrow. "Do I need to remind you of the ketchup incident?"

"That was one time and I was fourteen." How was he supposed to know that the top on the squeeze bottle had been loosened—except for his brother Macon who thought he was the king of pranks.

"Then there was the cherry pie—"

There was no way that should count. "It was a speed-eating competition. Of course I got messy."

"The mint chocolate shake incident," she said with a smirk he would have heard even if he couldn't see it on her face.

"Have you ever tried to drink a shake using a narrow paper straw? There was a chunk of mint chocolate stuck in the straw, and I had to get it out. I probably shouldn't have blown so hard."

"And then there is my personal favorite, the gyro."

Nash didn't have an excuse for that one. He'd been watching out for Macon while his mom and sister were looking at the Dylan's Department store Christmas window display and didn't realize, until it was too late, that the tahini sauce had dribbled out of the aluminum foil he'd failed to wrap properly around the bottom of the gyro. It had landed on his black fleece in three blobs like a delicious snowman.

He did not want a repeat of that when he was still hoping Chelle would say yes to changing their no-sex agreement. She already thought of him as a puppy. The last thing he needed was to look like he'd been rolling around in some deer poop out in the woods. Not that he would roll around in shit. It was a metaphor. Or a simile. Or a whatever the fuck she as a writer would know it was.

"Fine," he grumbled as he pulled off the fisherman's sweater.

"Who set up this date for your ridiculous bet?" she asked.

"There's food involved," he said as he grabbed a black turtleneck from the dresser drawer. "You know it had to be Griff."

"So how are things going? Keeping that marriage magic alive?"

"You know it's not real," he grumbled, more annoyed about it than he should be as he pulled on the turtleneck.

"Neither is my placement in a Hogwarts house," Bristol said, "but I still am Team Slytherin all the way."

"Don't be ridiculous. You're Gryffindor." Brave and strong, that was his kid sister, G house all the way.

He'd made sure of it, always hyped her up before her volleyball tournaments when their mom forgot to show and orchestra concerts that went on for fucking forever but still not long enough for their dad to put in an appearance. That's just what big brothers did.

"Not a chance, Hufflepuff," she scoffed.

The dumb things he did because his baby sister asked. "I should have never have agreed to take that stupid quiz with you."

"But you did, because you're a good big brother if a terrible dresser."

He looked down at his black turtleneck, smoothing his hands over the soft cashmere. "What's wrong with this one?"

"Just put on the navy blue sweater. It brings out your eyes. Women go crazy for that."

They did? He tugged off the turtleneck. "It's not a real date."

And maybe if you say it enough, Beckett, you'll stop wishing it could be.

"How would you know?" his sister snarked. "Your last date was what, a decade ago?"

Not quite, but it had been a while.

"I'm busy. I have responsibilities." He took out the navy sweater and pulled it on. "It's not easy helping to run Beckett Cosmetics while keeping you and Macon on the straight and narrow."

"Maybe you missed it, *Dad*, but we're both grown-ups now and our parents are doing better. Mom even remembered to pay the electric bill this month."

"Yeah, because I loaded her phone with enough reminder apps that she threatened to throw it out the window." It had been a whole ugly thing.

"But it works," Bristol said, her tone softening, "so maybe you take it as your sign to stop feeling like you have to always take care of us and you start taking care of yourself for once."

"I'm fine," he grumbled, ignoring the unease making his chest tight.

He was busy and fulfilled and had a ton of shit on his plate. There was no room for romance. Or feelings. Or finding the woman of his dreams.

"Then why is it so important to win this dumb bet?" Bristol asked.

"I have my reasons." Number one, being competitive was just in the Beckett DNA. Number two, it was all part of Grandma Betty's master plan of getting two-thirds of the oldest Beckett cousins to slow down long enough to fall in love. Her instructions that she'd left him in a letter to be read after her death had been clear. He had to play along so they wouldn't suspect anything and mess up their happily ever afters.

"Well, whatever they are," Bristol said, her tone making it more than crystal clear that, whatever they were, she thought they were dumb, "I think this marriage is good for you. It's an opportunity for you to step out of your comfort zone and stop acting like you don't need anything. It's okay to put yourself first sometimes."

"I see you're using that psych minor tonight."

Deflect? Him? Fuck yes. He didn't deal in feelings. He dealt in solutions.

"Well, you know they say the kids that take the psych classes only take them because they're fucked up."

"You're not fucked up." He picked up his phone and glared at his sister for thinking something so patently false. "You're perfect."

Her ever-present smile wavered a little at that. "I'm not, but you're sweet to say that."

Seeing her like this, vulnerable and a little unsure, kicked his big brother, let-me-take-care-of-it-all instincts into high gear. "All you need to do is—"

"Oh man, look at the time!" She held up her bare wrist as if she were wearing a watch, which she was not. "It's no mansplaining o'clock! Gotta go."

"Love you, Bristol."

"Love you, too, Nash," she said, back to her usual grinning self. "Now go out and have some newlywed fun with your sexy wife."

His sister ended the call before he could remind her—again—that his marriage was only temporary while reminding himself that he'd agreed to a sexless temporary marriage.

The other night had been a fluke. If it hadn't been, she would have said something to him during their dog walk, or breakfast, or when she'd gotten back from coffee with her friend, or a million other times over the past few days. Instead, she'd shut herself up in her room as much as possible and had gotten straight to writing her book, going by the clickity-clack of her keyboard.

Her silence was obviously her answer. He just had to find a way to live with that.

Chapter Twenty

Empanadas were the food of the gods.

"Oh my God," Chelle said, not even trying to hold back on her groan of appreciation. "This one wins. I thought it was going to be the falafel, but it's definitely this one."

"Well," Nash said as he scarfed down his second one, "don't forget to fill out your survey card, or Griff will hound you until you do."

She took another bite, the flavors exploding on her tongue as they stood there on the corner, during what had to be the best date she'd ever been on. A food truck crawl was fucking brilliant. "This place gets all tens."

"The survey scale only goes up to five," he said with a chuckle.

"Too bad." There was no way she was going to adhere to that rule for the best thing she'd ever eaten. Yep, that was her talking. She was a new, more daring Chelle Finch. "All tens."

Nash shook his head and tucked back the strand of her

hair that kept getting stuck to her lip gloss. "I think you're drunk on empanadas."

"I'm totally okay with that." And that little buzz of anticipation his touch set off in her belly.

"You'll have to be the one to tell Griff." He flashed the double dimpler at her. "He's a little rigid in a barely-talks, grumpy, LEGO-collecting scientist kind of way."

"Sounds like a character." Really, he'd have to be to agree to this asinine bet that she was totally going to get to the bottom of.

"He is," Nash said. "You'd like him. He'd definitely be an ogre in one of your books."

She paused mid-bite, all the warm and fuzzy getting doused with nervous dread, and waited for the passive-aggressive mocking that she'd gotten from her dad when she was younger about her, as he put it, "scribbling in her notebooks." There'd been the absent-minded questions, the warning her that there was no money in being an author, and the concern trolling that what she needed to be doing was finding a boyfriend (when she was younger) and then a husband (when she'd left for college) because that was the natural order of things. Her dad had told her, with all the condescending bullshittery possible, that was the way things worked for women. They had to find a man to guide them through life.

Fighting to keep her voice neutral as she prepped for the same from Nash, she asked, "So you made it through the first chapter, huh?"

He finished his last bite of the empanada, his body loose and easy. "More like I only have a few chapters left."

She watched him, waiting for him to add more, her body tight with nerves and the taste of bile replacing the delicious empanada flavor—but nothing came. It was probably just so he could get the timing of his supposedly well-meaning barbs right. She'd fallen for that trick before. They had come from her dad after he'd complimented something she'd baked and then commented on her weight, or from her uncle when he'd remarked about how many people the foundation had supplied with emergency housing funds and then followed up with a comment about how, if she wasn't so naive, she'd understand those people just needed to stop being so lazy.

None of that came from Nash, though. Oh, he looked like he wanted to say something, as if it was bubbling up inside of him—but he didn't.

"You're not gonna say anything else about it?" she asked, trying to adjust to this new reality. "Offer some constructive criticism? Plot advice? Share your detailed twelve-point plan to rework the second act?"

He made the motion of locking his mouth closed with an invisible key and then throwing it over his left shoulder.

The mansplainer had nothing to say.

Until he did.

He grimaced and let out a groan, as if he couldn't stop himself no matter how hard he tried. "You know, I know people in publishing. I can—"

She cut him off with a narrow-eyed glare. "No, thank you. My writing is just a hobby, something to do for fun. It's pure escapism. It's not like it's important."

"You are such a liar," he said. "I've seen how much you read. There's no way you don't think books are important."

Okay, he definitely had her there. But those were good books, amazing books, the kind of books that made people slow down their reading as they got closer to the end because they didn't want them to end.

"Fine," she said with a defeated sigh. "*My* book isn't important."

"Well, actually, it is." He hooked a finger under her chin and lifted it so that she had no choice but to look him in the eyes. "Important people create important things."

She waited for the snide follow-up, but there wasn't one—not from Nash. In fact, there never had been since they'd met each other. That's when she realized that even when he'd been mansplaining taking Sir Hiss on leashed walks or rearranging her furniture, he'd been doing it to help and not to put her in her place. The action may have been the same as the patronizing attention from her family, but the intent behind it couldn't be more different. That didn't excuse all of his well-actually bologna, but it did explain it. Nash really was trying to help. He was just making a royal fuck-up of the process.

"Are you buttering me up for something?" she asked, teasing him because it was easier than confronting how her discovery made her feel about him. "Is the next stop live worms served on fishing hooks with sriracha on the side?"

"Just stating the truth." He let his hand drop, flexing his fingers. "Come on, the taco truck down the street is the last one. It's only a few blocks, and then there's a car meeting us to take us home."

"Your cousins thought of everything—or was that you?"

He grinned at her and kept walking. "I'll leave it up to your very vivid imagination."

Yeah, she didn't need her imagination for this one. The guy who made her breakfast and then oiled her cast-iron pan after washing it to make sure it stayed seasoned wasn't going to forget a detail like arranging for a way for them to get home. Chelle had spent her entire life taking care of other people. That he thought ahead enough to make sure they got home safe gave her the warm fuzzies.

They started off down Canal Street just as the first snowflakes started to fall. It was one of those weird, almost full winter nights when it was cold enough to snow and yet it still felt warm for that time of year.

Or maybe, it was just walking next to Nash that did that.

Karmel's words about getting out of her own head and experiencing the buffet that was life went on repeat in her head. What if her friend had been right?

Really, what was the harm in giving it a try? A wild rush of anticipation went through her as she slipped her gloved hand into Nash's. He looked over and gave her a double dimpler, then tucked their clasped hands into the pocket of his coat, warming her whole body from the inside out.

And that's how they walked, neither of them acknowledging it out loud, the three blocks to the last food truck where they both got carne asada street tacos. They were good, but not nearly as good as the empanadas—and that would be true even if Chelle couldn't stop thinking about all of the what-ifs and how-this-could-works.

"So," she said as she balled up the paper her taco had been wrapped in and tossed it in the trash can, gathering up every last bit of her courage for what she was about to do next. "I've been thinking about your idea to change the no-sex clause in our verbal agreement, and I have a counteroffer."

For a second, Nash just stared at what was left of his third taco, and then he looked up at her with an intensity that sent a shiver through her. "Excellent."

"We scratch the itch." It was a logical proposal. "One time." What harm could there be in that? Right? Right. *Oh God*. What was she doing? "Get everything out of our system, and then we'll be able to make it through until Christmas without all of the unresolved sexual tension in the apartment."

And the tension on the street, in the stairwell, in the elevator, at the park—basically anywhere she was within ten feet of Nash Beckett.

He threw half of a perfectly good taco into the trash can and closed the distance between them. His jaw was rigid.

His entire body visibly tight. Suddenly, he wasn't a puppy anymore. He was all man. They stood there like that under the streetlight, half a block down from the taco truck, as a black town car idled at the curb beside them.

"Should we kiss on it?" he asked, his voice low and rough.

But he didn't make a move.

She got it. The next move was hers.

Part of her wondered if it was too late to take it back, but that was only a small bit, a sliver of nerves really. The rest of her was singing "Hallelujah" in all of its lusty glory. She went with that part, rising up on her tip toes, and kissed her for-a-limited-time-only husband like she'd been dreaming about doing since he'd kissed her at their wedding.

His lips were as hot as the snowflakes falling on them were icy cold. Then she slipped her tongue along the seam of his lips, he opened his mouth, and she realized that she hadn't had any fucking clue what hot was before this. The world turned into August on the equator as they kissed the hungry, needy kind of kisses that stole a person's breath and filled them with want. His hands were in her hair. Her body was pressed tight against his. Everything felt light and good and perfect.

Except for the fact that he had too many clothes on. Also, that she had too many clothes on. Then there was the fact that they were about a minute away from losing control and getting ticketed for indecent exposure—and possibly getting hypothermia—so she broke contact and stepped back.

"Get in the car, Chelle," Nash said, his palm on the small of her back as he hustled her over to the waiting sedan. "And don't even fucking look at me until we get inside your apartment or I can't promise you that I won't fuck you in the backseat until you come so hard half of Harbor City hears you."

Normally, she was more than sick and tired of having

to take orders from a guy who seemed to think he knew everything about everything.

This time was different.

This time she didn't mind at all because it was Nash.

And suddenly the phrase "temporary husband" started sounding like a curse instead of a blessing.

She was so screwed, and she didn't even care.

Chapter Twenty-One

The ride back to Chelle's apartment was pure fucking torture. The second the car dropped them off in front of her building, he let out a sigh of relief.

But it was too damn soon.

Before they could make it through the lobby, they got stopped by a woman named Suzanne who wanted to complain about Groucho Barks and Mary Puppins. He held it together long enough to admire the way Chelle shut the woman down, and then he hustled them up the stairs. Her door was just down the hallway, a yellow beacon representing the finish line where he'd get to strip her down and taste every inch of her—except for one thing.

Two things, really.

Two furry, yappy, and very happy to see them things that barreled straight for them as soon as they walked through the front door.

"Just give me a second to take them for a quick walk," she

said as she managed to clip on their leashes, even though the dogs were squirming like electric eels.

Yeah. No.

Nash scooped a leashed dog under each arm. "You get naked. I'll be right back."

Her eyes went dark with desire, and she didn't argue.

He would have thought the blast of cold air when he walked out the building's front door would have been enough to cool him off. He would have been wrong. He swore the snow was melting before the flakes even landed on him as he strode down the block.

"I swear, if you two take care of this fast, I will buy you each a lifetime supply of peanut butter–filled Kong toys."

Maybe they understood, maybe they took pity on him, or maybe they didn't want to be outside any longer than he did, because they were ready to go in a half block later. A cooler guy wouldn't have picked them up and all but sprinted back to the building and up the stairs. Nash was not that guy, though, not when Chelle was waiting for him.

He stashed the dogs in the kitchen with two bowls of kibble, made sure Sir Hiss had his dinner, double-checked there was water, and then rushed to Chelle's bedroom. He took a second to bring himself into check so he wouldn't look like one of her wild satyrs ready to fuck at a moment's notice, and then—fina-fucking-ly he opened the door.

The bed was empty.

Her bathroom was empty.

He highly doubted she was hiding in the closet, but like an asshole, he checked anyway.

That's when he heard her clear her throat, and he looked out into the hallway. Chelle stood in the open doorway of his room, wearing only a black, almost see-through robe and a shade of red lipstick she hadn't been wearing on their date. Dazed, he just stood there drinking her in, memorizing the way he could almost see all of her soft curves that made his mouth go dry. She toyed onerously with the end of her hair for a second and then set her shoulders. One side of her mouth tilted up into a smile as she curled her finger at him and then disappeared into his room.

No one needed to tell him twice. He strode across the hall and shut the bedroom door behind him. He didn't know where he wanted to look first. Her perfect tits nearly overflowing from the black bra she wore under the robe? Her hips that curved out in an exaggerated hourglass? The fuck-me red of her lips? The still a bit skittish but determined gleam in her eyes that promised he was in for a good time, but it wouldn't be easy? He doubted anything was with Chelle, and he more than appreciated that fact.

"I thought I told you to take your clothes off," he said as he crossed over to her, getting nearly close enough to touch her smooth skin before something in her eyes stopped him.

"Oh," she said with a sexy, husky chuckle, "you just want me in red lipstick and nothing else?"

"More than fucking life itself," he said, flicking open the top button on his jeans, so ready to torment her as hard as it seemed she was determined to tease him. "But why don't you sit back, have a drink, and let me show you how much?"

She sat down on the chair in the corner of the room where there was already an old-fashioned glass with a finger of whiskey waiting within reach. She picked up the glass and took a long drink before holding the glass in her lap with a tight grip.

Fuck.

He had no clue what was going on, but he had to make sure she was all in. "Chelle, are you sure you want this?"

"It's just been a long time and you're so much younger and there's no way that I look anywhere close to the women you're usually with and you don't want someone like me." She pressed her fingers to her lips. "I'm messing everything up."

"You could never do that, but you are one hundred percent wrong about one very important thing." He reached behind his head and pulled off his sweater. "I can't stop thinking about just how much I want you and what I'd like to do with you and to you. I don't want someone *like* you, I want *you*. But if you want me to stop, you need to tell me."

Cock hard as steel, he flipped off his shoes and then took off his jeans and underwear. The strip clubs weren't going to be calling him after that performance, but he didn't think slow was what Chelle was after tonight.

"Did you want a whiskey?" she asked, desire darkened her eyes as she watched.

"No." He shook his head as he wrapped his hand around his dick, giving it a hard, slow stroke, relishing the way she bit down on her full bottom lip as he did. "I'll have some of yours."

He let go of his cock and dipped a finger in her glass, then held it above the *V* opening of her robe and let the amber liquid drip off the tip and down the valley between her tits. Her moan of pleasure had him reaching down to squeeze the base of his dick to send the "slow down" signal to his balls.

This woman—this woman, at least tonight—knew exactly how to play him.

What she didn't seem to realize, though, was that he could play this game, too. Instead of bending over and licking her dry, he picked her up out of the chair and she gave out a surprised gasp. Then he put her down on her feet, and while she stood there, he dragged his tongue down the line of whiskey, licking up every drop as he stripped her robe off her and then let it drop to the floor.

She'd expect him to go for her bra next, to unhook it and let it drop. Too bad. Instead, he swept his tongue further south, kissing, licking, and nipping his way toward the promised land.

"I like your belly." He dropped a line of kisses that crossed just below her belly button. "And these hips are fucking fantastic." He glided his hands over her hips as he lowered himself to his knees in front of her. "I've been imagining your thighs so much." He rocked back on his heels and looked up at her. "Now it's my turn. I want to see you."

She bit down on her bottom lip as she trailed her fingers down the side of her neck and then moved them lower so they glided across the full, round curve of the top of her tits. "You want me to strip?"

"Fuck yes," he said, getting up and moving to the bed. Never looking away from her, he grabbed a condom from the nightstand. "I'm willing to beg, plead, whatever you want." He started to roll the condom on, his dick so sensitive already he was on the edge of coming. "Let me see you. Please."

He waited, holding his breath and his cock, and watched as she unhooked her bra and slipped it off. That's when things went a little glitchy in his head. Her tits weren't just perfect, they were something even better than that, and once he had blood going to his brain again, he'd ask her what the word for that was. She was the author, after all.

"God, you're beautiful." It was so true it was like saying the sky was blue or water was wet.

Then she took off her panties and stood before him in only that sinfully sexy red lipstick, and the world stopped spinning.

Fucking hell.

She was gorgeous, like a voluptuous sex goddess, all soft curves with a solid strength underneath that promised not only could she take care of everything, she'd also smite anyone who got in her way.

He'd never wanted anyone more in his life.

"Come here," he said, sounding as desperate for her as

he felt, as he sat on the edge of the bed, leaning back on his forearms.

She closed the distance between them, getting on the bed and straddling him before reaching between her legs and wrapping her hand around his cock. "Is this what you want?"

He'd thought he'd been hard before. He was wrong. Lust burned through him at her light touch and nearly undid him. "You are all I want."

She lowered herself down on him, enveloping him in her slick warmth, and started to ride him slow and steady, her big tits swaying as she moved. Her sweet mouth was open, her head tossed back as she took what she wanted, what she needed. The temptation was too much, and he curled the rest of the way up, threaded his hands through her dark hair, and brought her mouth down to his, kissing her with everything he had as her body rocked against his.

It was the best kind of torture, the kind that had him holding on to her, kissing her, for dear life as pleasure rolled through him in waves. It was good, so fucking good—but he wanted more. He wanted all of her.

Breaking the kiss, he grabbed her hips and stopped her in mid-downward thrust. She gave him a questioning look, but there was no time for her to say anything before he lifted her up and off of him, then put her on her back in the middle of the bed. Her dark hair was spread out and her legs were spread wide. Fuck, those legs, they were a sight to behold, full and thick.

"You're fucking beautiful," he said as he kissed his way up her inner thigh. "I could spend all night right here."

"Well, I hope you're going to go higher," she said, a ribbon of desperate need threaded through the words.

He grinned against her skin. "Impatient?"

"Right now?" She let out a shaky groan as he kissed that crease between her thigh and her pussy. "Very."

She lifted her hips, and he slid his hands underneath her round ass, supporting her and putting him in the perfect position to do exactly what he'd been dreaming about. He dove right in, licking and kissing her wet folds, devouring her, feasting on her like a man who'd been starving for only her his entire life and didn't realize it until that moment. He rounded her clit with his tongue, then lapped at it and sucked it as he slid two fingers deep inside, fucking her with them in a steady rhythm as he stretched her open.

"Nash," she moaned.

His name had never sounded so good before.

He teased her, taking her closer and closer before dialing it back a few notches, waiting to drag this out, let the pleasure build until there was no stopping it. Finally, though, she took back control, sinking her fingers into his hair and holding him in place as she rubbed against his mouth, demanding her due. He was all too happy to oblige, alternating between pressing his tongue against her clit and sucking on the sensitive nub until her thighs were shaking on either side of his head.

She came, her body arching, every part of her going as hard as he was. It was so damn hot, the tilt of her head, the sound of her pleasure, the way her whole body tensed before melting in his arms. Fucking gorgeous.

"Fuck me," she said a few moments later, still breathing hard.

"Is that rhetorical?" he asked and moved back enough to get a good look at her flushed body as she came down from that high.

She chuckled. "Not even a little bit."

"Good." He lined up his cock with her entrance and slid in one slow inch at a time, reveling in the feel of her wrapped around him until he was balls deep.

He stayed there for a second, trying to get ahold of himself as pleasure jolted his system and every part of his body tuned into the feel of being inside Chelle. Then she wrapped her legs around his waist and started moving her hips. What little control he'd been holding onto evaporated. He pulled back and thrust into her over and over as pure pleasure built in the base of his spine and his balls tightened. Fuck. He wasn't going to last long. It was too good, too intense, too everything.

"Chelle," he said in apology or warning, he wasn't sure.

She cupped his face so he had to look right at her as she moved her hips in tandem with him, taking him deeper as he thrust in and out of her. It was like a switch was flipped. He crashed his mouth down onto hers, kissing her as he kept pushing into her, fucking her with everything he had until it was too much, and his orgasm slammed into him, turning the rest of the world dark except for Chelle.

Only her.

She was everything.

Once the rest of the world came back into focus, he rolled on his back and got rid of the condom, dropping it into the trash can in the bathroom, then climbed back into bed and pulled her close. For a second, she hesitated but then with a soft sigh curled up against him, laying her head in the pocket of his shoulder.

"Don't go," he said.

"Are you sure?" she asked, her words brushing against his skin as he wrapped an arm around her. "That's why I came in here instead of my room. I wasn't sure you'd want me to spend the night here together."

"I will always want you to stay," he said. "Go to sleep, Chelle."

It wasn't until he was still staring at the ceiling a half hour later that he realized the truth of the words. It settled down through his chest, hitting him square in the heart.

"Oh shit," he grumbled to himself, then held his breath as Chelle mumbled something about having a magic potion before settling in to her steady sleep breathing.

He may have just been fucked, but he'd already fucked himself, because there was no way one time would be enough. Even worse, he was totally okay with that because being with Chelle—not just the sex, but actually being with her—was that good. Fuck that. Being with Chelle was amazing.

Outside, the snowstorm picked up, the wind making a sort of trilling sound when it hit the building that sounded a little too close to his grandma Betty's laugh for comfort. His mom would say that was a sign. For once, he had to agree with her woo-woo ways, because he knew in that moment, he had his first doubt that he wouldn't be winning the Last Man Standing bet.

And he didn't give a shit.

Chapter Twenty-Two

CHELLE

It wasn't like Chelle hadn't left her bed all week—she definitely had—it's just that she kept finding her way back there again and again and again. She blamed Nash's double dimpler. How was she supposed to think of anything but a naked him when he had that unfair advantage?

She couldn't.

She didn't.

She had no regrets.

So it was no surprise that she was curled up in bed with Nash when the outside world came knocking—literally—on her front door, in the form of his brother Macon and sister Bristol. While not exact copies of Nash, there was definitely a familial similarity with all three sharing killer dimples, the Beckett blue eyes, and enough height to make normal humans wonder what the world looked like from that perspective— even Bristol was six feet tall at a minimum. Of course, their looks weren't all they had in common.

"Are you all named after cities?" Chelle asked after everyone had pet the dogs, attempted to greet the cat who ignored them, and was holding mugs of fresh-brewed coffee.

"The place of our conception," Macon said, shrugging at Nash and Bristol, who both groaned. "Hey, if we have to be grossed out at the thought, I'm fine with sharing it."

"Maybe you are, but I don't mind keeping some of the mystery alive," Bristol said, rolling her eyes at her brother. "Or at least keeping the ugh-factor at bay."

Completely unruffled, Macon took another sip of his coffee as he shot an assessing look at Chelle and Nash. She sat on the chair where she'd looked at his sprained ankle the day they'd first met, while he sat on the arm of the chair, one huge hand cupping the oversize mug and the other touching her hair. For half a second, she fought that oh-shit-they-know embarrassment, the one that had always come with any hint of attraction that her dad would shame her for if he found out, and then she pressed back against the negative reaction. Instead of flinching, she allowed herself to relax against Nash's hip. It was a move that didn't go unnoticed.

Macon might have the look of a rich guy who had life handed to him on a silver platter—which come on, he was a Beckett, there was no way he hadn't—but there was more going on behind his baby blues than a lot of folks probably gave him credit for.

"Well," Bristol said, jabbing an elbow into Macon's ribs to really drive home the stop-staring-asshole message her glare was sending, "we've left you alone long enough. We're here to kidnap you and bring you and the animals to Mom's for brunch."

The mental image of her pugs having their usual bananas reaction to meeting new people and adding in the bonus—at least from the dogs' perspectives—of a new place to sniff around and ferret out every crumb and thing that they definitely shouldn't be chewing on was enough to make Chelle press her hand to her heart.

"I don't know that they're well behaved enough for that." But she did know. They most certainly were not.

Instead of nodding in agreement, though, all of the Becketts started laughing.

Chelle looked around from Nash to Bristol to Macon and then back to Nash. "What?"

"Mom has a demon chihuahua mix named Dudley who doesn't even pretend to be well behaved," Macon said. "Groucho, Mary, and Sir Hiss will be more than good enough to come."

Chelle was still trying to process that last bit, but her mouth rushed ahead of her brain. "You want me to bring the cat, too?"

"He's family, isn't he?" Bristol asked.

She'd always thought so, but other people looked at her like she'd grown a third head when she said her pets were as close to kids as she ever wanted. Okay, so she hadn't had that conversation with the Becketts, but it wasn't like she was going to be around them long enough to have to go through the conversation that had been the final nail in the coffin of her relationship with her dad. When she'd told him she didn't want kids, he promptly informed her that God had created women to be childbearing helpmates. She'd rolled her eyes so hard she was surprised she hadn't ended up with a permanent view of her brain.

"She's only a few blocks from here, and you know you want to give this another try," Nash said as he held up Sir Hiss's harness.

He wasn't wrong. Sir Hiss needed to practice his cat-walking skills.

Still...

She glanced from Bristol to Macon. "Only if you're sure."

"Mom will be thrilled," Nash said. "What do you think? Wanna go?"

And there it was. He was asking, not assuming what was right or pressing her with a mansplaining diatribe about why going to his mom's was the best option. It was such an abrupt change from their first day together that she didn't have words for it.

Maybe she could have resisted him even though every instinct in her body was telling her she could trust him, but add to that two additional pairs of double dimplers from his siblings who were nodding in agreement and she was a goner. It wasn't fair.

"Okay," Chelle said, still not quite believing this was about to happen. "Let's do this."

Nash took the dogs while she held onto Sir Hiss, and she only had to shoot Nash a warning glance once when he started to tell her the proper way to put a cat in a harness for him to back away from the dire pit mansplaining quicksand.

The weather had warmed up from their date night, but there was still a chill in the air as they walked to his mom's five-story townhouse right across the street from the eastern edge of St. George's Park. Bristol and Macon kept up a running commentary about everything from the gyro stand at the corner (killer food after a long day), the flock of geese that roamed the park (mean as their cousin Dixon when he lost at anything), and how to spot a tourist from ten stories up (the slow walking). Meanwhile, Nash held both dog leashes in his left hand so he could hold hers in his right, tucking them into his coat pocket to ward off the chill, while he just indulgently watched his brother and sister interact as if he was their proud dad instead of their older brother.

The difference in how their families interacted was stark. His obviously loved and supported one another. Meanwhile, she had an appointment with a judge coming up to prove that this temporary marriage fulfilled the draconian requirements of her dad's will and save the family foundation from Uncle Buckley. It was enough to make her whole body tense up with a mix of fury and nerves as her lungs tightened.

Nash shot her a questioning glance, but she forced a reassuring smile and breathed out the tension. She didn't want to ruin the easy companionship of the moment, and quite frankly, it wasn't like talking about her problems was going to do anything to change them. She just had to trust the judge would buy into her marriage that was starting to feel a little less temporary every time she looked at Nash.

By the time they got to the house where they'd grown up, Chelle's cheeks hurt from smiling so much at the by-play between Bristol and Macon. When they stopped, though, she had to do a double take at the Beckett townhouse. The stairs leading up to the front door spanned the width of the pale-yellow building ending at a grand landing with brown stones laid out to look like a parquet floor decorated with humongous pots of joyously red poinsettias.

They were halfway up and doing their best to keep the dogs from devouring the poisonous plants when the front door opened and a man who looked like a combo assistant/ bodyguard walked out. Tall, with short, platinum-blond hair and the kind of leathery perma-tan skin that spoke of decades in the sun—probably with baby oil, if she was guessing his age right—he watched them with amusement.

"Dudley will be thrilled," the man said as he squatted down and gave Mary Puppins and Groucho Barks the kind of level-ten scratches behind the ear that guaranteed they'd adore him for life.

"How's she doing?" Nash asked as they walked inside.

"Madame Celeste? She's had three readings this morning and has been anxiously awaiting brunch," he said, collecting the Becketts' coats. "She's cooking now."

"What?" all of the Becketts said at once, then rushed through the large, circular foyer and down the stairs, Groucho and Mary happily yapping and running along with them, Sir Hiss tucked into Nash's arms.

Chelle turned to the man obviously waiting for her coat, too.

"Chelle Finch," she said as she took it off.

The man lifted a perfectly sculpted eyebrow. "Chelle Finch-Beckett if I'm not mistaken."

"For the time being." Which was exactly why she shouldn't be feeling all warm and gooey on the inside right now or thinking about how nice Finch-Beckett sounded together.

"Well, Mrs. Chelle Finch-Beckett for the time being, I'm Bennie." He took her coat and hung it in the closet by the front door. "Just Bennie. Now"—he tilted his head toward the hall where the Becketts had disappeared—"let's go find out what disaster they found in the kitchen."

The kitchen was gorgeous, all commercial quality stainless steel, high-end countertops, and enough La Cruset cookware on every available surface to be the background for a streaming show about the cooking lives of the rich and famous. It smelled like heaven. In the middle of it all was Celeste Beckett talking a mile a minute as she moved from one dish to the next, mixing here, folding there, and adding spices everywhere. As she moved from one pot or skillet to another, Nash hovered behind her, handing her an oven mitt the moment before she grabbed a casserole dish straight out of the oven, obviously so distracted by trying to talk and hug her children at the same time she cooked that she'd nearly burned her hand off.

"Chelle!" Celeste called out the second she set the baking dish down on a purple trivet and spotted her. "I'm so glad we can have our first meal as a family. And you brought the babies!"

There really weren't enough exclamation points for how Celeste talked. It fit with the rest of her with her miles of bangles on her arms, purple-tipped dove-gray hair, and seventies Stevie Nicks witchy aesthetic. She wasn't like anyone else. She was absolutely 100 percent exactly who she was. It was both overwhelming and welcoming—kind of like the massive annual Bath & Body Works candle sale.

Returning Celeste's hug, Chelle looked over the older woman's shoulder and spotted Nash. His shoulders were tense. The double dimpler was nowhere in sight. He looked like he might crack a tooth, his jaw was clenched so tight. Macon and Bristol were near the huge island topped with a butcher's block counter, their body language rigid, but they sat back as Nash put out the metaphorical fires their mom set. It was obvious they loved Celeste—really, who would put in that level of work if they didn't—but it had taken its toll on all of them.

It broke her heart a little.

"Oh my goodness," Celeste said. "I'm so glad you came and brought all your fur babies. Now, let's go enjoy brunch."

Despite her realization, she did. Without having to watch out for their mom, Nash and his siblings fell back into their humorous give and take as they told Chelle embarrassing things he'd done as a kid, while Celeste talked about how he'd been such a serious boy growing up that it was good to see him smiling now. Then she looked at her eldest, and it was plain as day that for whatever else was true, Celeste Beckett loved her kids.

Families were so fucking complicated.

Luckily brunch, it turned out, was not. Once Nash had a chance to relax and enjoy the delicious food his mom had made, Chelle felt her own shoulders start to inch down. By the time they were back outside, ready to go home, pugs and feline leashed up beside them, she almost would have sworn that she'd imagined the whole thing.

"Hey, Beckett!" a man called out from the sidewalk.

They both turned, just in time to see a flash go off right in their faces. A freaked-out Sir Hiss responded by climbing Nash like a tree while the pugs lunged toward the photographer. Heart going a thousand miles an hour, she tightened her grip on the leashes and blinked away the giant white spots in her vision. Before Chelle even had a chance to process what was happening, Nash was guiding her and the animals into the park and putting as many people between them and the photographer as possible.

"Who was that?" she asked once their pace slowed down enough for a question. "Do you have your own paparazzi?"

His hand firm on her lower back, he led her around a particularly slow gaggle of tourists taking up almost the entire width of the main path through the park. "You really don't read the gossip pages, do you?"

She shook her head.

"Come on." He let out a tired sigh. "Let's hurry up and get home, and I'll tell you everything."

Chapter Twenty-Three

Yeah. Getting home fast didn't happen.

Instead, thanks to a painfully slow group of out-of-towners who were stopping every five steps to take selfies from about twenty-five angles each time, Nash and Chelle made a quick left at the path leading toward the pet café where they'd first met up. Unlike that day, though, it was packed with people and dogs of every size and shape—not to mention a handful of cats in walking harnesses similar to Sir Hiss's. Still, he managed to find them a table away from the path.

"So you know about the bet," he said after they'd sat down, gotten pup cups for Mary and Groucho and a hit of catnip for Sir Hiss, who was now as mellow as the orange ball of fluff was probably ever able to be.

"Yeah," Chelle said as she held her steaming cup of hot cocoa in her gloved hands. "It's kinda why we're married."

That reminder annoyed him more than it should, a

feeling he folded up and put in his back pocket before it could get out.

"Well, the gossip sites found out, and then someone made a TikTok, and after that all of the press attention just sort of took off." He sipped his hot cocoa with extra marshmallows and watched Chelle for any signs of familiarity. "You really had never heard any of this?"

She shook her head. "My For You Page is aspirational home DIY projects and thirst traps."

"Stay on that side of it, then." Except for the thirst traps. Fuck those guys.

"So, do people stalk you like you're famous or something?" she asked.

If this was famous, he would like to go back to being just another rich guy in a city full of them. "More like I find photographers outside my building when it's a slow news day."

She made sympathetic noises. "That sounds very not-fun."

"It could be worse." He picked up Mary's pup cup so she could better get to the goodness at the bottom. "I could be on the run from a veiled chimera."

"Ah," she said with a chuckle, "you've made it to book two."

Made it? More like he immediately started it as soon as he read the last line of book one. Like he even had a choice. There was no way he should be the only one reading her books. He'd already started priming Macon with hints about a great new unpublished author without giving away the fact that the author was Chelle. Yeah, he'd lied and told his brother that he'd found some really good fanfic, which there was a ton of, so that his brother wouldn't question how Nash had gotten his hands on an unpublished manuscript.

"I've gotten to the point where I kinda wish we could change from the mani-and-pedi date my cousins planned for tonight to reading by the fireplace," he said. Naked. Post orgasms. Maybe with some Thai delivered from that place around the corner from her building. "One of these would be clothing optional. Both would have champagne and strawberries."

"As tempting as that sounds, you do have a bet to win," she said, with a little too much forced cheer in her voice—or was he hearing that because he wanted to? "Are you ever going to tell me what the prize is?"

"We don't know." He shrugged at her exaggerated are-you-kidding-me look. "It's all part of Grandma Betty's plan. She knew the last thing Dixon, Griff, or I could resist was a competition. The next to last thing we could resist is a mystery. So when she died and her housekeeper Alexandra came to me with a letter from Grandma outlining her plan to get Griff and Dixon to find the women they'd fall in love with, I knew it would work."

Really, it was perfect. It was what both of them needed. Yeah, he didn't keep his mansplaining tendencies only to advice. Sometimes he used them for trickery—for the other person's own good, of course.

"But the thing is, you can't ever sell those guys on an idea by going straight at them. I've known them both my whole life and worked with them for years at Beckett Cosmetics. The only way to sell them on anything is to get them to think they're doing it because they're going to win and that they thought of the way to win all on their own."

"What about you?" Chelle picked up Sir Hiss, who was about as resistant as a bowl of Jell-O, and held him on her lap, stroking him under the chin as the feline purred as loud as a suped-up Corvette without a muffler. "Do you need to win?"

"Usually."

Her gaze dropped to the cat in her lap. "And this time?"

The correct answer should be absolutely. He had his

life figured out. He took care of his family, acted as the responsible older brother. He'd already gotten his cousins to fall in love and get started on their happily ever after. He didn't need that. He didn't want it. He didn't have time for it.

And yet, here he was about to confess that it was already too late for him.

But that's when Mary and Groucho started growling. His gut sank when he looked over his shoulder to see what had set off the dogs and spotted the photographer from earlier.

"Who's the girl, Beckett?" the man asked as he snapped pictures. "Guaranteeing you'll win that bet by picking someone like her. Smart plan. Lucky lady, what's your name?"

The photographer's words knocked Nash still for a second, and all he could do was stare at Chelle, her round cheeks pink from the chilly wind as her smile cracked and fell apart.

"Come on, honey," the man said as he clicked the shutter. "Give us a smile."

A savage rush of pure anger blasted through Nash, and he stood up fast enough that his chair fell back and clattered on the cement, setting off every dog in the café. He barely heard the barking, all of his attention was focused on the shithead who thought he could say anything to Chelle let alone the bullshit that had come out of his mouth.

Standing next to Chelle's chair, he loomed over the other man. "What the fuck did you just say?"

"Nash." She reached up and put her hand on his forearm. "It's not a big deal."

"The fuck it's not." He thought he'd been pissed before. That was nothing compared to the pure rage burning through him at the way the photographer's words had dimmed the light in her eyes. Then he'd taken in Chelle's slumped shoulders and the arm she'd put protectively around her middle as if subconsciously guarding against an attack, and he'd seen red. "It does matter," he told her, fighting to keep his fury in check. "I'm the fucking lucky one."

Her eyes went wide and some of the spark came back into her gaze—at least enough that he could turn his attention to the dirtbag who'd had the fucking audacity to say that shit to Chelle. The man continued to take pictures, but—obviously sensing danger—he'd put distance between them.

There were a million things Nash wanted to do, but he settled on the least violent. He ripped the camera out of the man's hands and took out the digital camera's memory card as the man backpedaled.

"I'll sue," the photographer spluttered. "You can't do this. It's my livelihood."

"I look forward to hearing from your attorney, assuming you can get someone to work with a slime ball like you." Nash shoved the camera into the man's chest, backing him up a few more feet. "You ever talk to my wife again like that and I will do a helluva lot more than this." He got his face right in the photographer's face. "Do you understand me?"

"Yeah, man. I got it."

"Good." Nash forced himself to take a step back before he gave in to temptation and beat the guy senseless. "Now get the fuck out of here."

He didn't have to tell the photographer twice. The other man hustled out of the café as people clapped and jeered and dogs growled.

For his part, Nash was all adrenaline and barely tapped righteous fury when he turned around and spotted Chelle standing by their table, the dogs sitting at her feet with their buggy eyes going opposite directions per usual and Sir Hiss sitting on a chair, casually cleaning the back of his paw.

Fuck.

This was not how this was supposed to go. As if brunch with his family wasn't overwhelming enough, he'd just lost it on a guy—who, yes, totally deserved it—instead of keeping his cool. That had never happened before. Not when the private school teacher had said that maybe if Macon's parents loved him, they would have showed up for parent-teacher conferences. Not when Bristol had started sleeping on his bedroom floor because of the nightmares after their parents started living hours away from each other. Not when both of his parents seemed to finally start seeing beyond their own self-centered but loving selves only to watch them fall back into old habits after a few weeks.

Only now.

And Chelle was staring at him like she'd never seen him before.

"Chelle," he said, shoving his hands through his hair as he braced for her disapproval. "I'm sorry."

"You should be." She tilted her head and pursed her lips. "I had my whole afternoon planned around writing a side quest scene, and now I can't decide if I want to write a sex scene or one where some asshole gets shoved off a cliff instead."

Relief sucked the tension right out of him half a second before he came up with the perfect solution.

"Well, actually, what you should do is act out the sex scene with me and afterward you get to fictionally kill someone who deserves it—not to mansplain your job to you, but you know it's a good idea."

"Well, actually," she said with a grin, "that sounds like the perfect plan."

And did he check his pace as they quick-walked back to her building to accommodate the dogs' tiny little legs?

Fuck no.

He carried the wiggly furballs the whole rest of the way home.

Quickly.

Chapter Twenty-Four

CHELLE

Chelle's apartment was too quiet.

Sure, if she counted the sound of the dogs tag-team snoring, it was the regular levels of loud, but this was different. This was there's-no-Nash silence, and she didn't like it. Honestly, it gave her the creeps. She couldn't even write, since part of her process was now blocking out the sound of Nash roaming through the apartment while he was on conference calls with his team, talking about Beckett Cosmetics product launches, sales figures, and potential distribution deals. The man could never work in a Panera, the staff would definitely kick him out for being disruptive.

It was true, but he was also *her* disruption, and despite having a mirror chat with herself about all the reasons why it was foolish—namely how this whole marriage of theirs was a total fake—she missed him.

She flopped down on the couch with a groan, and since she was already focused on the dumb things she was doing, she reached for her planner filled with all the details about the building Christmas party. She scanned the to-do list as her gut churned. Yep. It had definitely been a craptastic idea to suggest this. This was what happened when she decided that it would be fun to host a party. Eventually she had to actually have the party, which meant all of the work that went with putting on a party and—the worst part—actually interacting with people. Once she started chatting with her neighbors, it would be fine, but up until that moment, she'd be nothing but a ball of anxiety soaked in kerosene, standing by a lit match.

Note to self: never volunteer to put on a party ever again.

The dogs heard Nash's key in the door before she did, snapping out of a dead sleep to bound off the couch and rush to the front door. She shoved her planner aside, jumped up from the couch, and had checked herself in the mirror to smooth her hair into place and make sure she didn't have lettuce from today's lunch stuck between her teeth before he even cleared the foyer.

Damn, woman, what are you, some nineteen-fifties housewife?

She should be giving herself a serious talking-to about being this excited to see her fake temporary husband, but she was too excited to see Nash to go through the motions. He walked into the living room, the dogs yapping happily as they circled his ankles. And when he looked at her, all of the nervous energy that had been zapping her since he'd left for an emergency trip to the office this morning melted away as if it had never existed.

"Hey, honey," he said as he gave her a weary smile. "I'm home."

She was about to tease him about almost being late for dinner when she realized his smile was only a single dimpler. That couldn't be good. Then she looked closer at him, concern tightening her stomach. Nash looked exhausted—

well, as much as a hot guy in a custom-made suit could. His shoulders were slumped, his tie was askew, and he had the thousand-mile stare of someone who had seen some shit at the office.

"Do you want me to take the dogs for a walk?" He set his briefcase down with a tired sigh and then draped his suit jacket over the back of the chair, rolling his neck from side to side. "I can run down the block to the deli on the corner and grab sandwiches for us for dinner tonight."

"Dogs are walked and Uber Eats is already ordered." She crossed over to him and wrapped her arms around his solid middle. "Rough day at the office?"

"It always is when I get called in during the company's designated work-from-home time because that always means something went wrong—very wrong. We just closed a distribution deal with a chain of high-end and very exclusive boutiques in South Korea for months and things went sideways and—" He stopped and gave her an apologetic look. "Sorry, you don't want to hear any of this."

"Of course I do." She nudged him to sit down in the chair and took a seat herself on the ottoman. "Tell me everything."

He hesitated a few seconds, as though people didn't usually ask him about his problems, and they probably didn't. She'd met his family, and it wasn't that they didn't love him. They did. It wasn't like they ignored him like her family ignored her so much as they'd accepted that his part in the family was being the fixer. The thing was, though, who took that role for him?

Before she could ask him, he started telling her about his shitty day. As she undid his shoelaces for him and slipped off his shoes, he explained how an overeager intern accidentally deleted the boutique's orders from the system. Then everything went straight to shit after that, he told her as he wiggled his toes and let out an appreciative groan when she went to work rubbing the arches of his feet.

Chelle only got the general gist of things when he started using jargon and going into specifics about logistics. Then there was the part about skin serums baking out on loading docks because they'd been packed into regular shipping containers instead of refrigerated ones that sounded like a huge issue. By the time she finished his mini foot massage and the Uber Eats delivery driver rang the doorbell, he'd spilled about a million other fiddly little details that lead up to one pain-in-the-ass result—a trashed relationship with a distributor and a multi-billion dollar deal on the edge of disaster.

Their dinner order from Athena's Garden arrived at that part in the story. He went and changed out of his suit into his gray sweatpants and an Ice Knights T-shirt while she plated their spanakopita and poured a beer for each of them.

"So what happened next?" Chelle asked when he came back out.

He sat down across from her at the little bistro table in the kitchen. "Are you sure you want to hear more?"

She narrowed her eyes at him. If he even thought of holding out now when she had to know what happened next, she was gonna slide her always-cold hands under his shirt and plant her icy palms on his abs. That would serve him right.

"The intern had just sent a company-wide email that said 'Go tit!' instead of 'Got it,'" she said. "You can't leave me waiting to find out what happened next."

The double dimpler was back, and he continued the story, adding in little details about the people involved that made her giggle as he demolished the spanakopita like a man who'd missed breakfast and lunch, which by the sound of what his day had been like, he had. Without questioning, she got up and grabbed the two slices of baklava for dessert and put them both in front of Nash—they were medicinal at this point.

"Not only to everyone in the company but to the entire leadership team for the boutiques in South Korea." He ate the last bite of the savory spinach pie and let out a happy groan. "It was a giant fucking mess, but I fixed it." He shot her a cocky grin and started in on the baklava. "That's what I do." He let out a blissed-out sigh the second the honey pastry hit his tongue. "God, this is delicious."

"And what about the intern?" she asked. "Did you fire him?"

"Nah." He shook his head. "I worked with him on making a plan so this wouldn't happen again and told him I'd see him back in the office after the new year."

"You didn't even write him up?"

"I could have, but the guy has a lot of talent and drive. He was overeager, that's all. It happens," he said with a shrug, as if 99 percent of the people in his position at Beckett Cosmetics wouldn't have rained hellfire down on the intern without a second thought. "The important thing is that next time he's going to reach out to his supervisors before clicking submit on the cancellation form. He'll learn from this mistake, and hopefully, he'll ask for help before making another one."

"You're nicer than a lot of people," she said, meaning every word of it.

Sure, he still couldn't help but mansplain his way into trouble, but like the intern, he was trying. Nash Beckett was a pain in the ass, but he was a really good guy. The kind of guy she wanted for the heroines in her books—not perfect but solid. Who would have thought she'd finally find someone like that when the relationship was about as real as the fictional ones she wrote about?

"But," he said, interrupting the bittersweet turn of her thoughts, "not nicer than the woman who decides to organize a Christmas party for her whole building."

"You mean a glutton for punishment who now has serious regrets?" So, so many regrets. The kind that had her gut twisted up in knots.

He let out a protective, rumbly growl. "I take it Suzanne and your shitbag uncle RSVP'd a yes?"

She nodded and took her last bite of the spinach pie, crunching down on the flaky phyllo pastry. "But I've got plans for us tonight that have nothing to do with Uncle Buckley, the witch of the building, or Beckett Cosmetics deals on the brink."

His grimace transformed immediately into a cocky smile. "Does it involve getting naked?"

"Eventually," she said with a laugh. "But first you have to experience my favorite routine in the world. It's perfect for after a shit day."

"Okay," he said with an exaggerated sigh. "I'm game. What do I need to do?"

Chelle walked over to the couch and sat down. "Come sit down and put your head on my lap."

He waggled his eyebrows at her like some kind of cartoon playboy as he joined her in the living room. "I like where this is going."

Yeah, she kind of wished she'd come up with a different plan when he'd walked into the apartment looking like he'd taken on the entire world. However, she knew that this was what the guy who fixed everything for everyone else really needed.

"Keep your clothes on, Beckett."

He pouted, but he did what he was told, stretching out on the couch so his feet were at one end and his head was lying on her thighs. The dogs, obviously sensing a prime napping opportunity, jumped up and tucked themselves between the side of Nash's legs and the back of the couch.

After he had settled in, she used the home app on her

phone to dim the lights and start the gas fireplace. Then she opened up her audiobook app and hit play on her favorite comfort read, *Dead Until Dark* by Charlaine Harris. Yep, the best thing for a rough day was a little old school vampire romance. The book's opening lines came through the Bluetooth surround sound speakers.

"We're gonna listen to a book?" he asked, sounding like she'd just told him they were going to apply leeches to their bodies and let them drink them both dry.

"Yep," she said, not bothering to elaborate. "Now close your eyes."

When he did, she started running her fingers through his hair, slow and steady.

It didn't happen right away, but by the time Sookie started up her first conversation with vampire Bill during her waitressing shift at Merlotte's, the tension had ebbed out of Nash's shoulders. They sat there in silence for close to an hour, listening to the telepathic waitress's and vampire's story. It was so comfortable and so right that she sank back against the couch, her fingers tangled in his hair, even though she'd stopped dragging them through the strands and closed her eyes, too, soaking in the moment of absolute, perfect ease. Normally, it was just her and the pugs doing this, and it had always been magnificent. But with Nash? It was just better.

"I'm definitely going to hold this against you in the divorce," he said, his eyes still closed even after she'd hit pause on the audiobook an hour later. "You've turned my bones to mush."

"That's called self-care." She ran her fingers through his soft hair one last time because she was afraid if she didn't, she'd miss being able to even more when he was gone after Christmas. "I'll make sure to mention that in the divorce," she teased, desperate to lighten the mood that was starting to feel so heavy on her shoulders. "Judge, I was forced to wait

on him hand and foot and meet his many self-care needs."
This couldn't be about emotions. It could be about desire and
about mutual benefits, but it couldn't be more than that. She
wasn't sure she'd survive that. "And I know something that's
going to make it even worse."

"Oh yeah?" he asked, giving her a double dimpler that
made her heart flip-flop in her chest. "I can take it. Does it
involve getting naked?"

"Yes!" Orgasms were the perfect distraction from all of
these feelings trying to work their way up to the surface.

He was up and off the couch so fast that Mary and
Groucho started barking in surprise. She barely had time to
blink before he was scooping her up and carrying her out of
the living room and down the hall.

"Your place or mine?" he asked, looking from her
bedroom door to his.

"Surprise me."

And he did. Three gloriously toe-curling times.

Chapter Twenty-Five

CHELLE

The days after that night had been a whirlwind of writing and sex and watching Nash when he wasn't looking. He just fit in her apartment, with her pets, in her life, and it was messing up everything because their marriage was set to self-destruct.

Chelle had always loved disappearing from the everyday into her fantasy world, where satyrs and nymphs plotted to take down the gods and level Olympus down to the bedrock. Not anymore.

Now, instead of hearing her characters' voices in her head as they took the story from here to there every morning, she found herself listening to Nash singing silly, made-up songs to the dogs.

She'd also always loved the calendar featuring pics of cute rescue dogs in their new homes that hung right by her desk. Not anymore.

Now, instead of seeing sweetheart fluffer-doodles catching frisbees or playing tug, all she could see was

December twenty-fifth circled in red.

As a woman who'd promised herself that she wouldn't let anyone make decisions for her ever again, she'd relished the freedom of making choices based only on what she wanted to do.

Now, instead, of only thinking about her preferences, she took into consideration what Nash wanted, too, and how they could find a happy medium—say, for instance, the pan-African fusion restaurant they both loved rather than the Ethiopian place that she craved every day but was on his list of once-a-month places to go to eat.

Even worse, she didn't mind any of it—except for that date next week on the calendar. Oh sure, they'd agreed not to start divorce proceedings until after the new year, but Christmas was the end of it. No more movie nights where she missed half the movie because they got distracted by each other. No more waking up to the smell of fresh brewed coffee mixed with bacon and eggs. No more falling asleep with her head on Nash's chest as his breathing got slower and steadier, until it seemed like there was nothing in the world that could touch them.

Sleeping with him had definitely been a mistake.

It mixed everything up in her head, and now she didn't look at Nash and think *orgasms*, she looked at him and thought *home*.

Take this moment, for instance. Usually, she'd have her noise-canceling headphones on, listening to the same song over and over again while she wrote, but her headphones were across the room because she was listening out for the sounds of Nash coming home after an afternoon of putting out fires at his mom's house.

She was out of her seat a few minutes later, as soon as the dogs started barking at the front door.

She took a second to check her hair in the mirror above

her dresser before hustling out of her room. She angled her leg to block the dogs from escaping and reached for the knob.

"Hey there, stranger," she said as she opened the door, a welcoming smile already in place.

The teasing words were out of her mouth before she realized her mistake. It wasn't Nash standing on the other side of the threshold. It was Uncle Buckley in his trademark cowboy hat and never-seen-a-particle-of-farm-dirt boots.

"I know your marriage is just a farce, but I expected you to do a better job keeping up appearances rather than calling your husband," he made air quotes around the word, "a stranger. I swear, you aren't good-looking enough to be that dumb."

Even after years of being out on her own and out from under her father's patriarchal umbrella, her apology was at her lips before she realized it was forming. Clamping her mouth shut tight before it could slip out powered by decades of conditioning, she inhaled and exhaled a steadying breath through her nostrils as she reminded herself that their rules didn't apply to her anymore. She didn't have to accede to the men in her family just because. She was her own woman. She made her own decisions.

It took a second, but the urge to apologize subsided. "What are you doing here?"

"Seeing if you're ready to end these shenanigans yet," Uncle Buckley said, shooting a worried glance at the open space between the door and its frame as Mary and Groucho continued to growl from behind her.

"You're not getting control of the foundation." There was no way in hell. It helped too many people for her uncle's greed to win out. Just this morning she'd sent out approvals on a grant that would help with job training for folks staying at a domestic violence shelter and another for prepaid cell phones for those who were in dangerous situations but weren't yet ready to leave.

"We both know that's not true," he said, cocky and confident the way only an asshole could be. "Are you going to stuff those mutts in a closet and invite me inside?"

Chelle crossed her arms and didn't bother to wipe the *fuck you* off her face. "No."

"Fine," he said with a sigh. "We'll do this here, then. I have a judge ready to declare your marriage invalid for the purposes of your dad's will because it's all fake."

Her bravado disappeared in a flash as her stomach dropped all the way to the building's sub-basement and didn't make a rebound. It was like her entire insides were now just empty.

"If that was true," she said, fighting to keep the worst of the worried shakes out of her voice, "you wouldn't be here telling me this."

He shrugged his narrow shoulders. "This is an act of mercy. Give up now, and I'll allow you three months to wind down operations at the foundation. If you don't, everything will cease the minute the judge rules my way."

It was a bluff. It had to be. She already had an appointment set with a judge about the will. There was no way, even with all of the Finch family connections, her uncle could work around that.

But her roiled gut said otherwise. "I won't let that happen."

"Well, actually, it's not up to you." He held out an envelope that she reached for on automatic pilot. "Consider yourself served."

He slapped the envelope into her hand and stomped off on his cowboy boots, looking every bit as self-satisfied as a peacocking asshole could. That was it. She was definitely murdering a peacock shifter in her book.

Decision made, she stormed back into her room and sat

down at her desk, stuffing the court appearance notification into a drawer, annoyance and guilt eating away at her stomach lining. This was what happened when she paid more attention to fake worlds and fake husbands than reality. Now the people the foundation helped would suffer. If she hadn't been so busy with things that didn't matter in the long run, she would have realized that Uncle Buckley not being in her business the last couple weeks meant he was up to something—in this case, that something was setting up a hearing with a judge friendly to his side of things. If the judge ruled her marriage didn't meet her dad's requirements in the will, there were no other options. She needed to pull herself out of the made-up stories and make-believe married life and concentrate on what really mattered.

She was still seething quietly to herself ten minutes later, when Nash got home. He didn't stop to give the dogs a scratch behind the ears. He just came straight to her door, looking at her as if he needed to confirm she was still there. His blond hair was going every which way, like he'd been repeatedly shoving his fingers through it.

He took one look at her and grimaced. "So I guess you saw the pictures?"

Her stomach dropped all the way to her toes. *Pictures?* There was no way this was good. She shook her head.

"It's nothing." He gave her a smile, but it wasn't even a single dimpler. "It doesn't matter."

That was highly unlikely.

"Show me." Nash started to pocket his phone, but she nailed him with a do-not-fuck-with-me glare. "You do not get to make decisions for me. Only I get to do that. Let me see the pictures."

Reluctance obvious, he mumbled something to himself about just trying to help and handed over his cell. The photo he had pulled up was of the two of them at the pet café. It was taken at an angle that emphasized every oversize curve on her body, and the lighting had been tweaked *just so* on every one of the lines on her forehead, around her mouth, and branching out from her eyes. In addition, every gray hair on her head sparkled in the afternoon sun. She didn't look haggard, exactly, but she looked every one of her forty-two years and then a decade or two.

Whatever. It's what she looked like. She saw it every time she looked in a mirror. It wasn't a surprise or a shock even if it hurt almost as much as the headline above the picture.

HARBOR CITY'S MOST ELIGIBLE BACHELOR HEDGES HIS BETS WHEN IT COMES TO BEING THE LAST MAN STANDING WITH PLUS-SIZED MYSTERY SENIOR.

The sting of those words was so sharp it felt like a physical slap. She managed not to flinch, but reading it was still a big ouch. She would have liked to have said the headline didn't hit its mark, but no one knew better than a writer the power of words—especially when they were the truth.

"Don't worry." Nash swiped his phone back. "I'm already talking to my lawyer about—"

She stopped him with a wave of her hand. "It's fine."

"Chelle," he said with too much pity in his tone for her not to respond by throwing up an emotional wall.

"It's the truth, isn't it?" Did she sound as blasè as she was shooting for? No, but she'd power through anyway. "It's what we agreed to. You win the bet. I meet the conditions of my father's will. It is what it is."

A vein ticked in his temple as his jaw went rigid. "That's not all it is."

"For now." God, just saying that out loud was like having layers of skin scraped off with a rusty file, and she had to move away from him, putting physical distance between them like a practice run for what was inevitable. "We only have a little bit of time left and then that's all there is to it."

Something crossed Nash's face, the hint of an argument he was having with himself, and Chelle lifted her chin, daring him to fight with her. Honestly, it would feel good to get out all of the emotions swirling around in her. Fear. Anger. Frustration. Yeah, this was what she needed. A fight. A good, old-fashioned verbal brawl to decrease the pressure.

He crossed his arms over his broad chest and shook his head. "I know what you're doing."

Fire burned through her, eating away at the niceties and sharpening all her rough edges. "Are you about to mansplain me to myself?"

"Nope." He strode toward her, closing the distance in only a few strides. "I'm gonna do this."

Instead of opening his mouth and letting loose with all of the "well actuallys" and the "you knows," he scooped her up and carried her over to the bed, where he sat her down on the edge and dropped to his knees in front of her.

"Lift your ass." Feral. Demanding. Absolutely focused solely on her. "Please."

There was no way he could miss the fact that she was suddenly wet enough that she'd soaked the center of her yoga pants. But instead of taking that as a yes, he waited for her to make the next move. She had the power here. She could tell him no and he'd walk away—maybe a little bowlegged, but she had no doubts. He wouldn't try to bully her into doing what he wanted. He wouldn't demand his due. He wouldn't guilt her into fulfilling some role he'd perceived for her. It really was her call—and there was only one move she wanted to make.

Balancing her weight on her palms, she lifted her hips.

"If there's only a short time," he said, his low voice as rough as his movements as he yanked her leggings off and then tugged her down to the edge of the bed and shoved her thighs apart, "then I'm going to spend as much time as possible right here."

And when he finally lowered his head to the apex of her thighs, she had already forgotten about Uncle Buckley, the photos, the headline, and *everything* except for Nash.

Chapter Twenty-Six

NASH

The annual pre-Christmas decorating extravaganza lunch at Vito's Diner with his cousins was a Beckett family tradition—one that their grandma had started. Every year, the day before they went to decorate Gable House for the holidays, she'd gather all of the grandkids at the Harbor City diner for bottomless milkshakes and endless baskets of french fries. This being the first Christmas without Grandma Betty, Nash worried things would be a little quieter. He should have known better.

His cousin Morgan blew out a straw wrapper at Bristol, nailing his little sister in the head. "That is the absolute dumbest idea next to the Last Man Standing bet of theirs."

"You're full of shit," Bristol shot back as she crumpled the paper into a ball and launched it back across the huge, circular corner booth at Griff's younger sister. "Spending New Year's in Vegas under an alias is a brilliant idea—especially after you agree that the person who breaks character first has to host the family Fourth of July party."

"Why would you even want to take on an event you know is cursed?" Dixon asked, barely glancing up from the text messages he was getting from his fiancée, Fiona.

Bristol gasped. "It's not cursed."

Technically, probably not. However, in reality, the Beckett Fourth of July gatherings at the family beach house in Ocean Side were always a disaster—very entertaining, but always a disaster.

"Do you remember what happened with the fireworks display?" Nash asked, needling his sister enough that he was able to steal an entire fist full of fries.

"One time." Bristol held up a single finger for emphasis. "All of the fireworks were duds one single time."

"That's what happens when you buy fireworks from a guy who knows a guy who knows a guy who sells fake fireworks to suckers." Macon swiped more of her fries while she glared at Nash. "Then there were the sharks."

Bristol let out a huff of frustration as she curled her arms around her red plastic basket of fries and pulled it in close. "Come on, that is never going to happen again. An entire group of sharks just hang out on your strip of beach for a week, twice in one lifetime? Not gonna repeat."

"It's a shiver," Griff said, speaking up for the first time since Bristol had brought up the idea of a Come As You Aren't trip to Vegas and started trying to get Morgan to agree to spend one weekend in Sin City as someone—anyone—besides herself.

The whole table went silent, and everyone—including Dixon, who stopped giving his phone screen I'm-so-in-love cow eyes long enough to look up—stared at Griff. Seemingly oblivious to the stares, or more likely way too used to them, the usually silent, gruff cousin kept on dipping his fries into his chocolate milkshake before eating them.

After a few seconds, Griff's sister Morgan spoke up. "What's a shiver?"

"A group of sharks is a shiver," he said. "Don't forget the beach house haunting."

If Gable House was a quirky lake house with shrubs trimmed to look like geese, not to mention a real-life attack goose, then the family beach house was a creepy Gilded Age fear fest. It looked exactly like the location for a horror movie.

"Oh, come on," Bristol said, gathering up the few fries that hadn't been stolen from her basket. "That was Grandma Betty being Grandma Betty."

It was true. The woman always had a plot or a plan to stir things up.

"Could you imagine the amount of effort it took to set up that prank?" Nash said. "She had every corner of the beach house wired to set off ghostly encounters." All of the cousins had gone from room to room, trying to unravel the mystery, never realizing that it had been their grandmother all along. He chuckled, his whole chest going warm at the memory of her laugh when she'd finally revealed herself Scooby Doo-style by ripping off a Mike Myers mask. "There was no one like Grandma Betty."

Everyone nodded, silent for once in absolute agreement.

Nash raised his mint chocolate-chip milkshake. "To Grandma Betty."

All the cousins lifted their milkshakes and toasted the woman they all missed and then started up the smack talk again about the Last Man Standing bet and speculation about what was in the present from their grandmother. The guesses were getting more and more ridiculous, when Dixon cleared his throat and shot Nash a pointed look. Nash braced himself for whatever was coming next.

"So, Chelle's coming out to help decorate Gable House?" Dixon asked.

"Yeah," Nash said, trying to figure out what his cousins were planning. When Dixon had brought Fiona to Gable House for the first time, Nash and Griff had made sure they were stuck on the island in the middle of the lake overnight. Payback had to be in the works. "She's bringing her friend Karmel, whose show just wrapped for the season, and she's leaving right after to spend the holidays in Paris."

"You don't mean Karmel Kane AKA Violet Davis from the *Murder, She Wrote* remake?" Bristol's eyes had gone round, and she let out a fangirl giggle. "Oh. My. God. I love that show. I mean, I wouldn't want to end up vacationing in that little beach town and end up either dead or a murder suspect, but that is my Thursday night happy place."

Macon side-eyed her. "Murder is your happy place?"

"Don't judge me," Bristol said, pointing her fork—which still had a bite of waffle covered in dripping syrup on it—at her brother. "You are obsessed with picking locks—please don't tell me why, I like to have plausible deniability for whatever it is you're up to. Griff collects LEGOs. Morgan has that dumb planner thing. Dixon goes to bar trivia nights just to feed his need to win at everything. And Nash would explain how lightbulbs work to Edison. We're all weird."

Morgan flipped off her cousin. "Planners are not dumb."

"Yes, they are," everyone else at the table said at the same time.

Morgan rolled her eyes and snagged a piece of Dixon's cinnamon roll, popping it in her mouth before he could voice his objection.

"So is it *that* Karmel?" Bristol asked, already looking like she was planning all the selfies she was going to take with the actress in the background.

"That's the one." He shot his sister a warning glare. "Don't overwhelm her."

Bristol gasped dramatically and pressed her palm to her

chest. "I never overwhelm anyone."

Everyone at the table—even the usually silent Griff—laughed at that.

"Fine," she harrumphed. "I'll be calm and boring." She turned her attention to Nash. "But enough distraction. What we really want to know is that if Chelle is coming to Gable House to decorate for Christmas, does that mean you've already lost the bet?"

Before he could even form an answer in his head, Dixon let out a triumphant yell that got them stink-eyed by their waitress.

"If he has already lost, how are we going to figure out who gets Grandma's present?" Dixon said, no doubt already planning how he could be back in the running to win it.

"Rock, paper, scissors?" Macon asked.

"Imagine if you dorks would have just done that from the beginning instead of making this dumb bet," Morgan said with an I-told-you-so look at the three oldest cousins.

Dixon flipped her off. "Because then I wouldn't have met Fiona."

Griff flashed his cousin a smug grin. "Kinsey would have still been Morgan's roommate."

"But she never would have had a reason to pity date you," Dixon shot back.

Everyone at the table turned and looked at him.

"Grandma worked in mysterious ways," Nash said, not ready yet to let his cousins and siblings in on what was really going with him and Chelle, because he wasn't sure himself. "Don't think she didn't have a plan for you three. The younger cousins aren't getting away unscathed."

"No fucking way," Morgan said with a vehemence that left absolutely no doubt about how she felt. "There's no way I'm joining your Last Man Standing bet."

Macon and Bristol nodded in agreement as they finished

their breakfasts. After that, there was the usual fight for the check—one Nash always won because, while the rest of them were arguing amongst themselves, he had already given his credit card to the waitress before they'd even ordered. He took care of things. That's just what he did.

"So, here's the book I was telling you about," he told Macon as they pulled on their coats and walked toward the diner's door behind the rest of the cousins. "You need to read it right away."

"You know," Macon said as he took the thick stack of paper, "normally the author emails these things. No book agent gets an actual printed manuscript anymore."

"Yeah, well, it's important to take screen breaks." It was all true—and it was the perfect way to cover up the fact that he couldn't email the files to his brother because the files Chelle had sent were protected against anyone sharing them, if not printing. "You know, too much screen time can lead to eye strain, fatigue, and headaches."

His younger brother rolled his eyes. "Thank you, Dr. Nash."

"I'm just looking out for you." The *as always* went unsaid.

"And Chelle now, too." Macon ran his thumb across the edge of the stack, curving the pages' edges. "Does she know you're sharing it with me?"

"It's for her own good. She's really talented." All true.

His brother shook his head and muttered something that sounded a lot like *you dumb fuck* before saying, "Brother to brother, I have to tell you, you're walking on thin ice here. Writers are weird about sharing their work before they're ready."

Nash opened the diner door and walked out behind his brother into the cold, overcast December afternoon. "It's ready."

"That's usually the author's call to make, not their

husband who only married her to win a bet." Macon's eyes went wide. "That's what this is. You're trying to get her to stay." This time his younger brother definitely called him a *dumb fuck* under his breath. "There are better ways to win over a woman than to try and run her life."

"Just read the book," Nash said, shoving down the itchy feeling that his brother might be right. "I'm telling you, you'll regret it if you don't."

Did that sound like a threat or a promise? He didn't know or care.

Leaving the manuscript with his brother, Nash took off toward the park to avoid the pre-Christmas shoppers clogging up the sidewalks. He'd shave five minutes off the trip home by taking the walking path that went past the pet café. Chelle would just be wrapping up her writing time and getting ready to dive into her work for the foundation when he got home. Steps speeding up as he checked his watch, he figured he could play the timing right and stop at the deli on the corner to pick up a pack of her favorite Twizzlers.

He cut across the street to hit the shop on the corner across from the park, distracted by thoughts of Chelle and how fucking hot she looked in her writing uniform of messy bun and yoga pants. Nash headed into the bodega for Chelle's favorite writing food and a couple of sandwiches to have for dinner along with the soup he'd left simmering on the stovetop before he'd gone to brunch.

Macon was wrong about the book. If Nash hadn't given it to his brother, would that have been a better option? Chelle had kept the books hidden away for years, thinking— wrongly—that they weren't any good. They were fucking brilliant. But if he didn't share them with Macon, Chelle never would, and then she'd be trapped in that place where all she heard in her head was that she wasn't good enough. She *was*. She was amazing. She just needed a little nudge to get there. And if Macon didn't see how fantastic the books were, he'd never tell Chelle and she'd never get her feelings hurt.

That wasn't going to happen, but on the off chance his brother turned stupid overnight, Nash had protected her from ever knowing.

He grabbed a bag of strawberry Twizzlers and headed toward checkout, his shoulders getting lighter with each step closer to Chelle.

She'd be excited when she found out what he'd done, because his brother was going to love the book. Nash just needed to wait for the right time to tell her—the only problem being it was starting to feel like they didn't have enough of that left.

Chapter Twenty-Seven

CHELLE

Chelle was still trying to remember that the clock was ticking on this whole limited-time marriage, but it was hard when she was at Gable House with Nash and his family.

Fiona Hartigan—soon to be Beckett—had already gotten her to agree to be her date for the next Ice Knights game, since Dixon rooted for the hated Cajun Rage. Kinsey, who had a delicate engagement ring on her left hand, had tied a tea towel apron around Chelle's waist the second she said she'd help make the cranberry biscuits. The secret ingredient, she'd learned, was enough butter to clog every artery in Harbor City—in other words, the first batch was absolutely delicious. Griff had become best friends with Sir Hiss the moment the cat had landed on his shoulders, and the giant, tattooed guy grunted at him, then proceeded to ignore the feline completely as he worked on stringing the lights around the Christmas tree in the front room.

Meanwhile, Mary Puppins and Groucho Barks were

having the time of their lives out in the massive yard between the house and the lake, chasing after Maurice the attack goose, who was racing after Dixon, who was sneaking the huge bird squares of watermelon from a plastic baggie in his pocket while he added metallic red garland to the shrubs with Fiona's help. Bristol and Macon had teamed up to unpack all of the Christmas dishes their grandmother had collected while Karmel told them all the good gossip about everyone in Hollywood.

And Nash? Well, if he wasn't next to Chelle, using a water glass to cut out biscuits after she rolled the dough, he was checking on her pets, or sneaking kisses in the butler's pantry, or exchanging covert high fives with Alexandra, the housekeeper and knower of all things big and small when it came to the Becketts. The woman was a character, all regal silver hair and sparkling green eyes that never missed a thing. She'd given everyone their decorating assignments as soon as they'd walked in the front door of the brightly painted Victorian mansion. As a first timer, Chelle won the coveted job of putting the angels on all of the Christmas trees throughout the house.

And there were a lot—like fifteen—all with their own themed decor and filled with handmade decorations signed with one of the cousin's names and what grade they were in when they made them. She'd spent the last thirty minutes visiting each one with Nash, who carried a giant box of delicate angels that he unwrapped for her. His grandma had knitted each of the angels with such a soft touch and detail that they were works of art.

The Becketts were so different from the Finches that she had to keep reminding herself to stop expecting the worst, because unless the Becketts were complete sociopaths, their family was pretty close to the polar opposite of the one she'd grown up in. For one, the men weren't all in the den, drinks in hand, waiting for their wives to come refresh them. The women, in turn, weren't all packed into the kitchen or the laundry room, alone, doing the often unseen labor it takes to pull off a family gathering.

It was nice, and calm, and it would be easy to imagine that this was what her life would be like from now on—a large part of her wanted to live in the fantasy even knowing she had a few days to go before the timer went off on her marriage.

"I have a surprise for you," Nash said as he wrapped his arms around her waist from behind, tucking her in close so that the top of her head brushed the underside of his chin as they stood in front of the last Christmas tree.

"Does it involve a quickie in a closet?" Not that she'd been eyeballing the closed door under the stairs or anything—but she totally had.

Nash shifted his stance, bringing her closer against him. "No, but I like how your mind works." He spread his hand wide over her lower belly, sneaking a few fingers under the waistband of her jeans. "You know, I think we should try out all of the closets."

Was she tempted? Hell yes. Was she going to take Nash up on the offer? No. Getting caught going at it in a closet was not the way she wanted the Becketts to remember her, even if she'd likely never see them again after Christmas.

That little reminder had her blinking away unexpected tears as she stared hard—really fucking hard—at a badly cut-out stock-paper glove with a picture of Santa Claus drawn in crayon and signed *Nash, first grade*. Clenching her jaw tight enough to hurt, she inhaled a deep breath while making sure not to flinch or let her shoulders sink or in any other way show how hard the reality of the situation hit.

They had an agreement. She would stick to it. She owed him that much for helping her save the foundation from her uncle.

Pulling her shit together, she exhaled and did her best attempt at being casual. "What's the surprise, Nash?"

He stepped back, drawing his hand slowly across her belly as he did, as if he didn't want to let her go, either. Then he held out his hand to her. "Come with me."

"This better not be a closet," she said as she intertwined her fingers with his, a shiver of anticipation winding its way through her.

"Next time."

He led her to the door under the stairs, pushed it open, and stood back so she could see inside. At first all she could clock was how bright the room was with light coming in from south-facing windows that looked out toward the lake. Then she took stock of everything else in the room and her jaw dropped.

"Oh my God," she said, squeezing Nash's hand a little harder as she took it all in, trying to make sense of what he'd done.

What had been a small sitting room filled with several comfy-looking chairs bracketing a fireplace, had been transformed so that half of it was a near-exact replica of her writing space at home, right down to the same desk, a copy of her chair, and even the same brand of pens and notebooks that could only be found in a small, indie paper goods store in the Breakwater neighborhood that's business hours were basically whenever the woman running the shop felt like opening. There were even matching dog beds next to the desk so Mary and Groucho could nap while she worked. A laptop sat in the middle of the desk right next to a bright red one-cup coffeemaker. A black mug with THERE BE DRAGONS printed on it in gold was next to a basket overflowing with different-flavored coffee pods—exactly like it was at home.

Nash came up behind her, still holding her hand, and tucked her in against his hard chest, her head fitting perfectly under his chin. "I know you gave up your writing time to be here, and my family can be a lot, so I thought it would be nice to have this as a room to escape to or write if the urge hit, or you just needed to get away from the family this weekend."

Everything inside her went all gooey, and she had no clue how to process that. People doing things for her wasn't the way things worked in her life—at least not before Nash—so she focused on one thing that had nothing to do with emotions. "Is that my laptop?"

"No," he said, "but it's the same kind preloaded with the software and apps you use so you can log in and pick up where you left off."

Emotion clogged her throat, and she had to purse her lips together to keep the happy tears flooding her eyes at bay.

Had she thought laptops couldn't be emotional triggers? Obviously, that was before her fake husband had taken the time to get her a duplicate laptop to work on at his family's lake home.

And turned a sitting room into a replica of her office.

And held her against him while she tried to understand the jumble of happy, and excited, and terrified, and awed, and OMG everything fizzing around inside her like Pop Rocks.

Chelle didn't know where to look, her gaze ping-ponging from one thing to another as an unfamiliar warmth blossomed in her chest until it felt like she might burst. Instead, she turned in his arms, pulling back just enough that when she tilted her chin up, she could see Nash as he chewed the bottom of his lip.

"Look, I know it's not exactly the same, and looking at it now, it's a little creepy. I swear I'm not building a shrine to you in a basement somewhere." He let out a hard exhale, then looked down at her. "Do you hate it?"

And just like that, everything settled in her chest, a certainty that changed absolutely everything.

"I don't hate it," she said. "Not even a little."

Sure, she was talking about the double office, but deep down she knew that wasn't all she meant.

Deep down? Really? Honey, maybe a few millimeters below skin level if we're really gonna swing for the fences. You're into Nash Beckett. Fuck that. You love him.

She would have argued with herself if she could—but she couldn't. She'd completely fallen for her fake husband a few weeks before divorce proceedings were scheduled to start after New Year's. She had two choices.

One, cry about it.

Two, pretend time could be slowed down just like in one of her books and that day would never come and enjoy the next week.

There really wasn't a choice, though. She might regret it later—she totally would—but that was for tomorrow. Until Christmas, she had Nash and she wasn't about to waste even a moment of the next few days. So she curled a finger in one of the belt loops of his jeans and started walking backward into her office, tugging him with her.

"In fact, I need to show you just how much I don't hate it, right now."

Nash grinned at her, his hands already reaching behind his head for the collar of his sweater while he kicked the door of her office away from home shut behind them.

• • •

Chelle hadn't realized that laughing so hard wine went up her nose was an actual thing that could happen in real life, but here she was sitting in the den after dinner with her nostrils burning from the Bottle Rocket California cabernet she'd brought, unable to stop laughing even with the pain.

Bristol was standing in the middle of the living room,

a half-filled glass of wine in one hand and two Thin Mint Girl Scout cookies she'd won from Macon in a round of rock, paper, scissors in the other. She wasn't weaving exactly, but her wine was sloshing a bit from side to side in her glass. Every time Macon went to go refill it, Nash glared at him with absolutely no sense of subtlety, to the point that Bristol just flipped her oldest brother off and held out her glass and told story after story of Nash's less-successful exploits.

"So there's Nash," Bristol said as she tried to control her giggles, "standing in the canoe as it slowly sinks into the lake, holding Maurice above his head as the panicking goose flaps its wings and honks as if it's being murdered, all because the delusional animal really does think it's a guard dog that happens to be afraid of water."

The room broke out in laughter. Judging by the mock pained expression on Nash's face as his lips twitched with the effort to suppress a smile, though, he was okay with the teasing, and she hadn't heard him even start to mansplain even though she could tell he was dying to explain to his siblings all of the hangover hell that was awaiting them the next morning.

"But," he said as he dropped an arm across the back of the couch where they sat, "I won the bet."

Bristol's head dropped back and she let out a long-suffering groan. "You three and your pathological competitive streak." She lifted her head back up, crossed her arms, and managed to glare at all three of the oldest Beckett cousins at the same time. "You really need to talk to someone about that."

"I'm perfectly happy with winning all the time," Dixon said as he added another log to the ginormous fireplace.

From his spot at the chessboard across from Morgan, who was kicking his ass, Nash's brother Macon scoffed. "You didn't win the Last Man Standing bet."

Dixon glanced over at Fiona sitting on the faux bearskin

rug, putting together a puzzle, and smiled. "I most definitely won."

Fiona rolled her eyes but matched his sappy grin as she got up and made her way over to her fiancé, then gave him a kiss. "And so have the Ice Knights. I think us going to every home game has brought them luck."

The oldest of the Beckett cousins grumbled under his breath something that sounded a lot like "go Rage," but that didn't dim the obvious love in his eyes when he looked at Fiona.

"You have something you want to add?" Bristol asked her cousin Griff.

The big guy with his tats and shaggy beard sitting next to his fiancée on the pillow-packed window seat just grunted.

"Let me translate," Kinsey said, her Southern accent as thick as honey. "His life changed for the better the day he met me, and not only because of my family cornbread recipe. Plus, he never cared about the Last Man Standing bet from the moment he saw me and got knocked out." She snuggled up against Griff. "Did I get that right?"

Griff said something low and rumbly that only Kinsey could catch, but whatever it was, it turned her grin from bright to blinding.

The younger trio of cousins started throwing white cheddar popcorn at the happy couples and making gagging noises, but there was no sly cruelty in it, no barely concealed sarcasm, no unspoken censure. Instead, there was love, a sense of family, and the accepted knowledge that each of these people would always be there for the others. It was almost more than Chelle could process.

Knowing her family was toxic was one thing. Being part of a family—even if only for another few days—built on love as opposed to absolute obedience was something so completely opposite from what she'd experienced. The shock of it clogged her throat with a mix of bittersweet emotion—happiness for Nash even as she mourned what she'd never had. She hoped he realized how lucky he was.

Twirling one of her more gray than black strands of her hair around his finger, he snuggled in closer to her. "You okay?"

"I don't think I've ever been better."

God, she wished she was lying—but she wasn't. Being here with Nash and his family in this big Victorian lake house with an attack goose on duty...everything felt right, the way it usually only did when she was writing about satyrs and nymphs and love conquering all.

Of course, that only happened in her books.

In real life, she was a woman on borrowed time in a marriage that had been defined by an immutable sell-by date, and there was no way to revise that ending to anything close to a happily ever after.

Chapter Twenty-Eight

NASH

Chelle was already pulling away, and it was gutting him.

He'd been watching her all day, the boulder of dread in his gut getting heavier and heavier as he saw it all unfold. It was all there in the faraway look she had in her eyes during dinner, the sad smile she shot him during the goose story, and the soft sigh she'd let out while they sat on the loveseat and watched the fire turn to embers after everyone else had turned in for the night. So he'd taken her hand—he couldn't help himself, being near Chelle and not touching her was pure torture—and led her upstairs to their room, promising himself that he'd start disengaging from the fantasy that all of this was real.

But not tonight.

He'd give himself one more night to show her how he felt, since there was no way he could tell her—she deserved better than to be put in that kind of awkward position of having to find a way to tell him she didn't feel the same.

He opened the door to their room and stepped back, letting her enter first. Damn, he loved watching the woman move. The way her round ass filled out her jeans was a sight he was never going to forget.

"Are you just gonna watch me?" she asked with a sexy pout.

He strolled in after her, putting on that cocky smile that she always responded to. "Maybe."

Then he sat down on the bench at the end of the bed and did just that as she turned completely and made her way over to him, until she was standing between his legs, her full tits and her hard nipples poking against her thin sweater. When she grasped the hem of it, he held his breath. He fisted his hands on his thighs to stop from reaching up and doing it for her, because for as much as he wanted to rip it off of her and feast on her until she was writhing with pleasure in his arms, he wanted to slow every moment down—make time stop.

She had other ideas. She lifted the dark blue material, inching it upward at first, only showing an inch of the white skin of her soft stomach, then it was her see-through black bra and her pale pink nipples. By the time she swept it upward off her head and gave him the full view of her amazing tits curving above her bra, he was hypnotized.

Chelle hooked a finger under his chin and tilted his face up. "Close your eyes."

"Why?" he asked, blinking as he tried to work out the logic of it.

Her lips tilted upward in a small, sly smile. "Because I want you to do more than just see me."

"Trust me, I do," he said. "Actually, I—"

"Nash," she cut in. "Close them."

He did what he was told.

In an instant, everything went black as he fought the frustration of not being able to watch her, memorize every line, every freckle, every millimeter of her. It locked his lungs tight and made him clench the muscles in his ass as he fought every instinct, every want, every need to have all of Chelle and to take care of her.

She stroked her thumb across his jaw, her touch feather light. "Breathe, Nash."

Fuck. He was messing this all up.

"Nash." The air moved around him as she leaned in close, her warm scent encircling him. Then her lips brushed his earlobe. "Please."

He exhaled the breath he'd been holding, and Chelle came into being on a whole new level. Check that. She came into being on a million different levels. It was more than just her scent that tied itself in ribbons around him. It was the half a second of tightened anticipation as he sensed her before she touched or kissed him. It was the way, when she trailed her fingers down the front of his sweater before reaching the hem and tugging it up over his head, that it imprinted on some primal part of him. The nearly overwhelming pleasure as she glided her palms over his bare chest that shot straight to his dick. Then she kissed her way down the side of his neck as she braced her hands on his thighs, and he felt her lower herself down between his legs. The second she undid the button of his jeans, he was already at the breaking point.

With his eyes shut tight, he was surrounded everywhere by Chelle. She was every inhale and exhale, every anticipated second, every hope and want and need mixed into the wife he never wanted to give up.

"Stand up," she said, sounding as on edge and desperate as he felt at that moment.

He didn't hesitate.

While her taking off his sweater had been slow and deliberate, she yanked down his jeans and boxer briefs in one fluid motion. He had just enough time to register the cool air on his hard cock before it was surrounded by the warm, wet heat of her mouth.

"Fuck," he groaned out as she took him in deep, until he hit the back of her throat.

He dropped his hands to the top of her head, winding his fingers through the silky strands of her hair, and she hummed her approval on his cock as he pumped his hips. Her hands were on his ass, her fingernails imprinting on his skin as she met him stroke for stroke. Her tongue, her lips, the pressure as she sucked him in had him on the verge of coming before he was ready. His eyes snapped open, and the sight of Chelle with his dick in her mouth as she looked at him had his balls tightening.

Fuck that.

"You're coming before I do."

She pulled her mouth off of him but kept slow-stroking his dick. "You opened your eyes."

"Good try," he said as he scooped her up and tossed her on the bed, "but you're not changing the subject."

He stripped her jeans and panties off before she had a chance to respond. Whatever she was going to say morphed into a gasp of pleasure when he sank between her splayed legs. Forget teasing or drawing it out. He wanted her to come hard and fast all over his mouth, so he went after it like a man desperate to show how high they could go together. Tuned into the way her body responded—the hitch of her breath, the moment her thighs started to quiver on either side of his head—he cupped her ass and lifted it up off the bed, changing the angle until he hit right at the perfect spot, and she started begging him not to stop. She didn't have to worry. Stopping was the last thing he was about to do, because all he wanted in the world was to make Chelle feel good.

"*Nash*," she cried out as she came.

Her breathing was still erratic when he rolled on a

condom, climbed up onto the bed, lifted her up, and lowered her down on his hard cock. Holding her hips, he moved her up and down as she came back to herself, her lust-hazy eyes clearing somewhat but that satisfied smile of hers staying in place.

"You wanted to watch, huh?" she asked as she leaned forward, dangling her full tits just above his mouth.

He didn't answer. He didn't need to. Because the truth of it was that he'd always want to see her, to feel her, to be with her. This wasn't just a good time until he won the bet and she went to court to confirm she'd met the requirements of that crazy will so she could save the foundation from her jackass uncle. This was so much more. It was everything. Chelle Finch was everything—and he'd never be able to get her out of his system. He didn't even want to try.

The realization hit him a half second before his orgasm sucked all of the air out of his body, and the last thing he saw before pleasure forced his eyes closed was the woman he loved.

This was where he was meant to be—with her, always.

And it was the last place he'd get to be after the divorce proceedings started.

A few minutes later, Chelle was curled up on Nash's chest, with his arms wrapped around her while they watched the snow fall outside the window in comfortable silence. Silence wasn't normally his thing. There was usually too much he needed to say to make sure things were taken care of, that no one forgot anything, and to give someone the information they may not have even realized they needed. But with Chelle? He could lay in the bed, quiet, and know that these kind of moments with her were about as good as it could get.

He could relax.

"What were Christmases here like before?" she asked, her voice soft and quiet as she traced a swerved pattern across his chest with her fingers.

"You mean with Grandma Betty?"

Chelle nodded, and a million images flooded Nash's brain. Decorating the tree. Chasing down Maurice so they could include the goose in the annual family Christmas photo. Eating the dozens and dozens and dozens of cookies that Grandma Betty ordered in from a local bakery. Spending Christmas Eve pretending to sleep in a huge blanket fort with his cousins, brother, and sister, and laughing so hard at the dumb jokes Macon made that chocolate milk came out of Nash's nose. It wasn't just that the Christmases were fun, it was that it had been one of the few times growing up when he wasn't on duty, watching out for his parents, Macon, or Bristol.

"They were amazing."

"Your family is pretty great." She propped her chin on the back of her hand pressed to the spot above his heart and looked up at him. "Is this always a cousin thing, though? None of your parents are here."

Nash let out a weary sigh before he could stop himself.

"Shit," Chelle said as she scrunched up her nose and squeezed her eyes shut. "I hit on a sore spot? Sorry. You don't have to say anything. It's not my business."

But he wanted it to be her business, just like he wanted all of her headaches to be his. He brushed a kiss across her temple and circled his palm over her bare back as she sprawled over his chest. "It's okay, I want you to know."

She comically opened only one eye and, squinting up at him, asked, "You do?"

"You're my wife."

Her lush lips flattened into a thin line as she pressed them tightly together, and she dropped her gaze to the base of his neck before letting out a shaky breath. "We both know that's only true for the next few days."

"But it's true now." He stopped himself before he could let out a promise that it would always be. She wasn't ready for that. He needed time to bring her around. Unfortunately, he only had a few days. It wasn't enough, but it would have to be.

So instead of saying all of that, he glided his palm up and down her spine in slow, reassuring strokes. "This has always been a cousins-only event. I think Grandma made it that way because she knew none of our parents are exactly parents-of-the-year material. Dixon's are probably the closest, but they've definitely got their reasons for not being here. Griff's mom is dead and his dad is a true piece of shit. My parents fit somewhere in the middle. They love Macon, Bristol, and me, but they have their own way of showing it."

When a person was with either of his parents, it was easy to feel like the center of their world, but as soon as they were out of sight, they were out of mind. It wasn't personal. It worked the same for money or meetings or friends.

"Both of my parents grew up without a real concept of how to get things done in the real world, about the importance of paying bills when they were due, or getting forms for school signed, or all the logistical stuff it takes to make a household function. They're good people, but they need someone to take care of that for them."

Chelle kissed his chest above his heart. "And that someone was you."

"Yeah, but I don't mind." Sure, sometimes it was exhausting, and he'd skipped out on trips or experiences or even owning a fish because he couldn't take care of *one more thing*, but that's just the way it was for the responsible, oldest child. "It's just easier that way, and I can make sure everyone is taken care of."

She lifted her face and looked up at him, a smile teasing the corners of her mouth. "That explains your mansplaining."

He stopped mid-stroke, feeling a bit like the room had gotten brighter somehow. "I like to help."

"And who helps you?" Chelle cocked her head in question and pursed her lips, as if trying to stop herself from saying something else.

"I'm fine," he said, the words coming out more defensive than they would have usually. "I've got everything and everyone taken care of."

Chelle let out a soft sigh and snuggled against him, so there really was no daylight getting between them. "You're a good guy, Nash."

It wasn't "I love you." It wasn't "I want to make this fake marriage real." It wasn't *forever*. Not yet. But he'd figure out how to make that happen over the next few days. He had to. There was no way he could sit back and watch Chelle walk out of his life for good.

Chapter Twenty-Nine

Two days later, Chelle was back home with Nash, both of them in ridiculous matching pajamas with cats in Santa hats, blasting the holiday hits playlist while rethinking her choice of buying silver tinsel that now seemed to be everywhere *except* hanging from the branches of the sad, little, droopy tree that had been the last one left at the corner stand. Tinsel was in her hair. Sir Hiss had stolen clumps of it, piling it up in the highest part of his cat stand. Mary Puppins had enough of it on her to look like she was wearing an avant-garde doggie outfit.

So yeah, tree trimming this year was pretty much chaos. Chelle couldn't be happier about it—and no, that wasn't the spiked eggnog talking.

Standing by the archway dividing the living room from the kitchen and watching Nash dance—badly—and sing—off-key—while holding Groucho Barks tucked up against him like a football as he tossed strands of the devil's paper, Chelle took a moment to soak in the domestic bliss of the moment. Focusing on the ridiculousness of Nash shaking his perfect ass to "Jingle Bell Rock" made it easier to pretend this was her life, now and forever. And when she did that, she didn't have to think about the fact that Christmas—and the end of their marriage—was only three days away. Oh sure, they'd give it until after New Year's because who wants to file for divorce in the dead space between one holiday and the next, but as soon as the Christmas tree Nash overwhelmed with tinsel was on the curb, her marriage would go in the bin, too.

All of the conditions had now been met. They'd had their six dates, starting with IKEA, then the tabletop games, food truck crawl, the mani/pedi, decorating Gable House, and tonight, picking out the perfect Christmas tree. That hateful summons from her uncle still sat in her desk drawer, but she'd talked to a lawyer and he'd agreed Nash's plan of a temporary marriage still counted as a marriage for the sake of the will. He was confident the judge, even one who golfed with her uncle, would agree. The foundation would be safe.

She should be happy, thrilled, ecstatic. She had gotten everything she wanted. And yet there was a large nugget of coal sitting in her stomach, weighing her down.

She took a gulp of spiked eggnog, letting the burn of whiskey going down pull her away from the edge of regret before she did something stupid, like asking Nash if he wanted to make this marriage of convenience a real one. He'd probably say yes just because he wanted to help her—he'd be her pity husband. He couldn't help himself. If he thought there was advice he could give or an action he could take that would make someone's life easier, he offered it up.

The thing was, though, that she didn't want anyone with her because they were just being nice or thought they were fixing her life. She wanted someone with her because they couldn't imagine being without her. She couldn't blame Nash for not feeling that way about her. He'd always been honest about what this marriage was—and what it wasn't.

Three days.

Seventy-two hours.

Then the lawyers got involved.

Her phone buzzed on the bookshelf.

UGH. So that's where I left it.

She'd been in the middle of scrolling through emails, looking for an update about Uncle Buckley's latest ploy to get a judge to declare her marriage didn't fit the requirements of her dad's will, when she'd distractedly put her phone down because Nash came out in his cat pajamas. Really, how did he manage to look so hot wearing a clothing ode to festive kitties? It wasn't fair.

Her phone vibrated again. She picked it up off of the stack of Shelly Laurenston books that had changed her thoughts about honey badgers forever and glanced down at the screen.

Pulse pounding, she read the text from her lawyer again. And again. And a fourth time just to really make sure it said what she thought it did.

"What's wrong?" Nash asked, setting Groucho down and hurrying over to her side.

If she could have formed words without the truth tumbling out, she would have. Instead, she turned her phone so the screen faced Nash as she worked to keep her outward demeanor neutral. There was no reason to let on that she was—in a weird way—disappointed.

"Well, that's good news, right?" His shoulders a twelve million on a ten-point tension scale, Nash rubbed his palm against the back of his neck and kept his attention focused on her phone. "The judge sided with you on the marriage. Nothing in the will stipulated how long you had to be married. That's great. It's perfect. It—"

Is fucking awful, a voice screamed in her head.

"Is exactly why we did this," she said instead of letting that voice out. "Thank you for helping me save the foundation from my uncle."

That was the important part. The fact that all she wanted to do now was curl up into a ball under the Christmas tree and listen to "All I Want for Christmas is You" on repeat while eating badly decorated sugar cookies didn't matter. Keeping her gaze averted until she could get the whole blinking away her suddenly watery eyes thing out of the way, Chelle took a deep breath, trying to get herself under control. This was exactly what she'd wanted from the beginning. This was what they'd agreed to. The fact that she'd fallen in love with him didn't change anything. This was the perfect reminder that all of this—right down to the obnoxious silver tinsel she'd still be finding the remnants of in the corners and crevices in her apartment this summer—was part of an arrangement. It wasn't real, no matter how much it had become real to her.

"Well," Nash said as he took his phone out of his pajama pocket, "I was saving this for Christmas, but if we're celebrating, we might as well double it."

He tapped the screen a few times and handed her his phone. She scanned the email from his brother, looking for Nash's good news. It wasn't until the third sentence that she realized this email wasn't about Nash at all. It was about her. More specifically, her books.

I know the perfect editor for Chelle's book. I went ahead and had an off-the-record discussion, and they are rabid to get their hands on it. I gave the editor a few sample chapters and they're ready to make a six-figure offer—more if Chelle agrees to sign a deal without taking the book to auction. We need to set up a meeting ASAP.

Everything inside Chelle turned cold and quiet, as if

she'd just jumped into the icy lake behind Gable House and had sunk to the bottom. The Christmas music went away. The happy yapping of the pugs silenced. Even the sound of her furiously beating heart and the pounding of her pulse in her ear was muted. Emotional muscle memory honed by a lifetime with her father and his men-know-best ways took over at that moment. The coldness insulated her from the fire-hot pain of Nash doing what she never thought he would.

How could you be so stupid, Michelle? You knew better. From the very first moment you met him, he told you exactly who he was—a mansplainer.

But she'd seen him up close for weeks now, and she'd let herself be fooled. All this time she thought Nash was different—better—than the other men in her life, the ones who tried to control her life right down to her ability to do the job she loved at the foundation that made a difference for so many people. Now Nash was trying to control the other part of her life that had always only belonged to her. Her stories. Her fantasy worlds. Her *escape.*

A weary sigh escaped as she handed Nash his phone. "You gave your brother my book?"

"I knew he'd love it!" He wrapped his arms around her in a bear hug, lifting her up off the ground and spinning her. "This is amazing, right?"

"Yeah, amazing," she said, a hot ember of anger starting to defrost the numbness.

Nash put her down, shooting her a double dimpler as he grabbed her hand and pulled her into the kitchen. "So, you don't have to sign with Macon as your agent, obviously, so don't stress about that." He stopped in front of the fridge, opening it and getting out a bottle of champagne that she hadn't bought. "If you want to stay with him, though, he's really good. He reps a lot of big authors. If you don't, I'll take care of it. You don't have to worry about anything."

She yanked her hand out of his grasp, not bothering to keep her anger out of her tone. "Not even if I want to submit my book for publication."

Nash paused in front of the open cabinet, where he'd been reaching for two champagne flutes, his dimples disappearing as his smile flattened into a grim line. "Actually, it hasn't been sent to an editor yet. All of that was unofficial chatting, because Macon doesn't officially represent you yet."

"Oh, you didn't decide that for me, too?" she asked, each word as brittle as she felt at that moment.

"I don't understand why you're mad." Nash set the champagne bottle down on the counter as the dogs circled his feet. "This is a good thing."

"Uh-huh," she said in that tone, the one a woman gets in that moment between her heart breaking and the actual pain of it hitting, gutting her and leaving her empty. Groucho's and Mary's ears perked up at the sound, and they scurried out of the kitchen, their tails tucked. "And when I gave you copies of my book to read, what did I tell you?"

Nash crossed his arms over his broad chest. "Not to give feedback, and I didn't."

Who in the fuck was he to take a defensive posture here as if she was the one who was wrong?

"I also told you that I didn't want to publish them," she said, fighting to keep the emotion out of her tone and off her face. "They aren't ready."

"A publisher is ready to pay a million dollars for it," he said, throwing his arms up in the air, his frustration as obvious as the vein bulging in his temple. "I'm pretty sure that means it's ready."

"And you know best, right?" God, why did this hurt so much? She should shut up, not give in to the hurt and heartache that would let him label her as hysterical or overreacting, but she couldn't help herself. All of it just came pouring out in strained sentences that pushed their way through the emotion making her throat raw. "I'm just the silly woman who needs to get out of the way when it comes to making decisions even if they involve me? It's a good thing my dad put that clause in his will or who knows what I'd be up to."

"I am not like your dad," he all but roared at her.

"Really?" she scoffed, pain streaking through her entire body like a million electric shocks. How could she have been so oblivious to what had been right in front of her face the entire time? "Did you not just make a major, life-altering decision for me, not only without any of my input but by doing something I'd expressly said I didn't want?"

"This isn't like that," he said more calmly this time, reaching out to her. "I was just trying to help."

She sidestepped, avoiding his touch as she locked eyes with him. "Yeah, well, I think you've helped enough." She stalked over to the front door, each step stiff, and pulled it open. "You got what you wanted out of this. Six dates. No falling in love. You're going to win your Last Man Standing bet. I got what I wanted, and my uncle can't force me out of the foundation and close it. We both have everything we ever wanted so, actually, it's past time we called quits on this whole marriage charade."

He started toward her, his hands up in supplication. "Chelle—"

She shut him up with a glare. "For my entire life, men have been telling me they know what's best for me. There was my dad and the bullshit clause in his will requiring me to get married. Then there was my uncle trying to maneuver me into accepting my real position in the world as a helpmate for my husband." She sucked in a breath, blinking away the tears threatening to fall. She would not let them. Later, when she was alone, she wouldn't fight it, but not now, in front of the man she'd fallen in love with, the one she thought saw her as capable, worthy, an equal. "Then there's you, deciding what the best thing was for my books. I've had enough. Go home, Nash—your own home."

Shoulders slumped, face down, he walked over to the door, stopping long enough to give the two dogs scratches under their collars. Then he let out a defeated sigh and looked up at her, his own gaze watery.

"I won't do it again," he said, his voice breaking. "Please... give me another chance."

"Nash, you've been doing this your entire life. It's who you are. You can't help but help people—even when they don't need it or want it." She couldn't stop the tears now. They slid down her cheeks as fast as she wiped them away with a hard scrub of the back of her hand. "Please, just leave."

He took one last look at her, as if he was memorizing every last detail, and then walked out her front door.

It was exactly what she wanted.

It was exactly what she knew would happen.

And it was the worst moment of her life.

Chapter Thirty

NASH

The next morning, Nash woke up in his own bed in his own apartment in his own neighborhood after a shitty night's sleep mostly spent glaring at his ceiling and wondering why in the hell the silence here was so much louder than at Chelle's place, where there was always a dog barking or snoring or panting after having the zoomies. He made a pot of coffee and realized after he'd already hit start that he only needed a single cup. It was the same story with the too many eggs he'd scrambled and the extra bacon he'd cooked and the fact that after breakfast he went to his cookie jar, looking for the dog food that had never, ever been there.

But that had been where Chelle had kept the kibble at her place.

He just stood there staring at the neatly organized shelves arranged according to meal, not something ridiculous like color, like Chelle's bookshelves, for God knew how long until someone started pounding on his door. Since he lived in the penthouse with a private elevator someone needed a key to operate, he knew who was at the door before he even opened it and found his sister on the other side.

"I got your text," Bristol said as she walked in, worry forming a *V* on her forehead as she looked him up and down. "What happened?"

He'd texted last night to let her know that he had moved back into his own place. It wasn't because he wanted sympathy or—God forbid—to talk about what happened with his little sister, but because he needed to make sure she knew where to find him if something came up. The last thing he wanted was for her not to be able to reach him if she needed his help.

He started back toward the kitchen. "It's not worth talking about."

"Translation," she said, following him. "It very much is."

"Do you want some eggs?" When his sister shook her head, he turned on the kitchen faucet and started washing the skillet, scrubbing it until it practically gleamed. "Chelle's writing a fantasy series about these woodland nymph assassins and the satyrs that are their mortal enemies and lovers." There was no way that they should be forgotten about in some folder on her laptop. Even the idea of it was wrong on so many levels. The books didn't just have potential like the Door Dash guy's customized sneakers. They were exactly the kind of stories that stuck with people like peanut butter on a spoon. "They're really fucking good, so I shared the first one with Macon and he told an editor about it and they want to make a big-ass offer on it."

"That's amazing," Bristol said as she poured herself a cup of coffee.

Finally! Someone got it.

"That's exactly what I told her." He dried off the skillet and flipped the dishtowel over one shoulder.

"Why does it feel like there's a but coming?" she asked.

Unease creeped up his spine, the itchy kind that usually made an appearance about five minutes after he did something like explain how multi-leashes worked to a dog walker or offered advice to a couple arguing on the A Train. That oh-shit feeling, though, couldn't be right. Not this time. He'd only been looking out for Chelle and her future, not butting in where he wasn't wanted.

"The but is that now she's pissed I shared the book with Macon," he said. "She doesn't want to publish them."

"How could you have known—" Bristol stopped mid-sentence, closed her eyes, and let out a long sigh. "She told you that, but you ignored her because you thought you knew better."

"I told Macon to read Chelle's book because it's that good." He started pacing from one end of the massive granite island in the middle of the kitchen to the other, needing some way—any way—to shake off the uncomfortable feeling that he'd screwed himself out of any chance he had to make his fake marriage a real one. "She just can't see it. I was helping her."

Just like he helped his family. He was always the one with the answers. Always the one who knew what to do next. Always the one who took care of everything. If he wasn't that, then who in the hell was he?

Bristol shot him an are-you-completely-oblivious-to-your-own-bad-ideas glare. "You know there is a big, thick line dotted with red flags between being helpful and taking over, between showing someone another perspective and insisting your way is the one way, between giving insight and mansplaining someone's life to them."

"You're wrong." She had to be. There was no way that he would have ruined everything by being right.

"I guess congratulations are in order, then," she said, sounding anything but congratulatory. "With this development, looks like you just might win that stupid Last Man Standing bet of yours, then." She paused, taking a sip of coffee as she watched him over the rim of her mug. "It's too bad, though. I really thought you two had something."

Nash didn't even have to try to picture his life as it had been a day ago on that last date. They'd debated the benefits of one sad-looking Christmas tree over another with the fervor of an old married couple picking what show to watch on TV. Then he'd tossed it over his shoulder and carried it home while Chelle walked beside him with the dogs, who stopped every three steps to sniff a mailbox or the corner of a stoop. It had just started to snow when they got to the corner of her block, and she'd stuck her tongue out to catch the flakes, managing to look both adorable and hot in the process. When she'd opened up the package with matching Christmas pajamas, he hadn't hesitated, because he'd known it would make her smile and there was nothing better than that.

Yesterday had been perfect, right up until it hadn't.

"Our marriage was just an arrangement," he said, each word feeling like a lie. "As Chelle said to me yesterday, we both got what we needed out of it."

Bristol sat her coffee mug down on the island, sympathy shining in her eyes as she gave him a grim smile. "Whatever you say, Nash."

What he'd said was the cold, hard truth—no mansplaining needed.

Chapter Thirty-One

CHELLE

Chelle left the dogs at home this time as she trudged through the fresh-fallen snow along the dog path across St. George's Park to Grounded Coffee for a meeting she wasn't sure she'd ever be ready to have. Some things a grown-ass adult couldn't skip out on, though, and that included firing the agent she'd never hired in the first place.

As soon as she entered the coffee shop, Macon waved at her from a table in front of the glass wall looking into the kitchen, where the chefs were making mouthwateringly good chocolate croissants, hazelnut puffs, and other pastries.

Clearing her throat still raw from a night spent crying, she walked over and sat down across from him. The waitress lingering nearby sending Macon not-so-covert glances was at their table a second later. After taking their order, she hurried to the kitchen, and Macon launched into a cheerful congratulations and deep dive into his expectations for her book and the pros and cons of taking the deal that would be offered, as opposed to putting the book up for auction so several publishing houses could fight over it.

It was amazing and overwhelming and not the conversation she needed to be having with him right now.

"Look," she said when he finally took a breath and she pushed past the awkward humiliation of the moment burning a hole in her gut. "I know you did all of this as a favor to your brother, but you don't have to worry about it. I'm not interested in publishing the book."

Macon just stared at her for a second, his jaw hanging open. Then he planted his forearms on the table and leaned forward.

"Please tell me you're kidding." Concern formed a deep *V* on his forehead. "I mean, I understand if you want to go with another agent, the whole brother-in-law as your agent thing could get messy, but you did me the favor by writing this book. I haven't been able to stop thinking about it."

It had to be bullshit. He was just setting her up for the sandwich method of real compliment, passive-aggressive shiv to the heart, followed by an insincere compliment. Her father had perfected the move and she'd learned to guard against it even if it still always managed to cut her deep. However, Macon didn't follow up with anything else. He just sat back and drank the coffee the waitress had delivered.

"You mean the offer wasn't just put out there as a favor to you or Nash?" Chelle asked, trying to process what was happening.

"Publishing doesn't work that way." Macon snort-laughed and adjusted his glasses. "Okay, celebrities and politicians get massive book deals that no one expects to ever earn out, but a debut author doesn't get that kind of deal no matter who they might be married to."

A hot flash of excitement mixed with terror and a hefty dose of denial rushed through her, making her hands shake, so she wrapped them around her vanilla latte but didn't lift it, because she didn't trust herself at the moment not to drop the whole thing in her lap. "I'm sure you're just being nice."

He narrowed his eyes at her as he tucked his shoulder-length hair behind his ears, the move revealing colorful tattoos peeking out from beneath the cuffs of his shirt. "Chelle, have you read your book? The publisher knows what I know. You're the next big thing, something even a guy like Nash, who usually only reads business books, could see. Please tell me there are more books in the works."

"I have two more finished, and the fourth book is almost done," she said almost too quietly to be heard over the din of the coffee house chatter.

Her lack of volume didn't faze Macon, who looked like she'd just given him the Christmas present he'd been wanting for his entire life. "Are you ready to do this? Because I am."

"I'd never really thought about being a writer for real." Embarrassment set her cheeks on fire. Even the idea of being vulnerable with someone enough to tell them about her books would have been too ridiculous to consider a few months ago, but then she met Nash and everything changed. Still, it was hard for her to wrap her brain around. "It's just something I do for fun. I can't leave the foundation to be a writer."

"No one's asking you to," Macon said, calm confidence wafting off of him like Axe body spray on a teenage boy. "Nothing needs to change on your end of things. Continue on as the foundation's executive director and write the books on the side. You get the best of both worlds." He paused and grinned at her. "All you have to do is say yes."

Chelle walked home in a haze. It was like she'd left the coffee shop, blinked, and was back home with Groucho and Mary happy yapping at her ankles while Sir Hiss watched from his spot at the top of the bookshelf. Her mouth was open to call out to Nash when she remembered he wasn't here anymore. She'd kicked him out, and he'd gone, which was exactly what both of them had needed to happen. Their partnership had reached its logical conclusion, and she was damned if she'd let another man make life decisions for her.

Fine. He may have done her a solid by sharing her book with Macon, but she wasn't ready to actually agree to that. He had done it without her permission. She'd thought he'd changed his take-charge mansplaining ways, but he obviously hadn't.

Yet, a stubborn voice inside her head whispered.

God, why was everything so confusing, and why did she miss him wandering through the house as he held conference calls, his voice booming down the hall and interrupting the flow of her writing? Why did she keep standing in the doorway to his room, staring at his bed? Why had she picked up her phone at least half a dozen times in the past day, ready to call him but chickening out at the last minute?

The whole marriage thing had just been a means to an end. Sure, she'd fucked up and gotten close to Nash—maybe even thinking she'd fallen for him, but that couldn't be real. Pacing through the living room, trying to get ahold of herself as her thoughts spun out, she automatically veered a few inches to the left to avoid the coffee table. But the table wasn't in that spot anymore. Nash had realized she'd bumped her shin on it on a near-hour basis and had moved it over.

Staring at the coffee table now six inches to the right of where it had been, her throat clogged up with emotion again. Damn it, she would not start crying again. What she needed was a massive distraction, an escape, a hole to open up in the middle of her living room and suck her into another world.

Wait.

She actually could go somewhere else and get lost without ever leaving her apartment. Her book! Chelle was almost done with book four, and getting back to it as her nymph assassin heroine took out the evil wizard would be the perfect escape for the mix of happy and sad sloshing through her.

She gave Groucho and Mary each a chew bone while Sir Hiss got a new catnip-stuffed plush carrot, and then she went to work. Everything at her desk was how it was supposed to be. Journals—half of which were blank because they were too pretty to write in—and pens on her right. Coffeemaker and pods on her left. Laptop dead center with her manuscript pulled up to the big climactic fight scene.

Yes. This was what she needed to get out of whatever funk was starting to descend whenever she realized something else that felt off because Nash wasn't there. Writing had gotten her through the pain of growing up a Finch. It would definitely dull the ache of missing Nash.

It had to.

Three hours later, with enough caffeine in her system to superpower a dragon, Chelle reread her sixth attempt at the battle to end all battles. Then she let out a groan of defeat and let her head fall to her desk, her forehead landing on her keyboard and probably doing a better job of writing this book than she was.

Where there should have been swords clanging in an epic fight between good and evil, her main characters just ended up kissing. Heavily. And then getting naked. That was definitely not good battle etiquette.

When her heroine was supposed to deliver a rousing speech to her troops, she ended up declaring her love for the satyr who was her sworn nemesis, right up until they decided that their shared enemy, the wizard, was worse and they had to join forces to defeat him. That was not supposed to happen until at least book five.

And then, when everything was supposed to go sideways and it would look like all was lost, instead of coming together for one last underdog attempt at winning, the nymph and satyr sacrificed themselves for the other, leaving them both mortally wounded on the battlefield, holding hands as their troops seized victory.

There was only one explanation for it. Her brain was broken.

"Fuck me and the horse I rode in on," she groaned.

"Well, that sounds exciting, but I'm just here for our catch-up before my car for Paris gets here, so time for a writing break."

Chelle let out a scream and jumped out of her chair.

Karmel chuckled and held up a bottle of Bottle Rocket rosé, the extra set of keys to Chelle's apartment jingling in her hand. After lowering her oversize black sunglasses, she looked down the hall toward the other bedroom. "Where's Nash?"

"Gone." She sank back into her chair, too deflated to stay standing.

"Gone?" Karmel asked, both of her eyebrows going high enough to get lost behind her cheaper-than-a-facelift bangs.

Chelle nodded, her gut twisting. "Gone."

"Tell me everything before my car gets here." She glanced down at her phone. "We have half an hour."

Yeah, that was more time than it would take to tell her best friend that her fake marriage had gone to shit. Still, she led Karmel into the kitchen, where Chelle opened up the wine, filled each of their glasses with more than enough to match the need of the circumstances, and spilled her guts, managing—somehow—not to go all sniffly, even though she could feel her nose start to tingle and had to do a bunch of blinking to keep the tears away.

"So you said yes about the book deal, right?" Karmel asked after topping off her rosé.

Chelle shook her head.

Her friend gasped. "You said no?"

"I said I needed to think about it." And then she'd all but run out of the coffee shop, not that she planned on admitting that out loud to anyone any time soon.

"Hardball. I like it." Karmel clinked her wineglass against Chelle's. "So, what do you really want?"

"I don't know," she said with a sigh, then drained the rest of her glass.

Karmel scooped up Mary Puppins and put her in her lap, then stroked her head with just the right amount of pressure to make the pug's bulgy eyes close with delight. Of course, while Mary was basking under Karmel's touch, her friend's clear-eyed and determined focus was centered on Chelle. Her stomach did a flip-flop thing, and she knew that whatever was about to come next, she probably wasn't going to like it.

"Is that why Nash isn't here anymore?" Karmel asked.

"No." Her chest became uncomfortably tight as she tried to find the words to make her friend understand that she hadn't had any choice. She'd done what she'd had to do. "He totally crossed the line by giving Macon my book even though he knew it was for his eyes only."

"And that was wrong." Karmel pursed her lips together as though trying to figure out what to say next. "But is it unforgivable?"

Yes. No. She didn't have a fucking clue.

"It doesn't matter," she said finally, the tip of her nose starting to tingle again. "This marriage was never meant to be real."

"Uh-huh." Karmel took a sip of wine. "It sure looked

real from the outside. Did it feel real?"

"No." Chelle's hands shook as she poured herself another glass of rosé, giving her an excuse to keep her gaze focused on the task at hand, as opposed to her bestie who would most definitely know she was full of shit.

"Lie to me if you have to, but don't lie to yourself."

What was the point in trying to fib to either of them? They both knew the truth of it. Despite it all, she'd fallen for her fake husband.

"He just would have done it again, ignoring what I wanted or needed because he thought he knew better," she said, her voice barely above a whisper. "I mean, not only would he share my book, but he'd think he knew what was best for me better than I did."

Karmel sat Mary Puppins back on the floor and reached across the table to cover Chelle's hand with her own. "Just like your dad?"

"Exactly," she said, all the raw feelings coming to the surface and making her want to put as much distance between herself and anyone who could hurt her like that. "I can spot all the signs from a million miles."

"Is it that, or are you just expecting to see them and so you do?"

"That's not fair," Chelle huffed.

"Some would say you aren't being fair, either." Karmel squeezed her hand and shot her a sympathetic smile. "Look, I love you like my own sister, and you may not want to hear it, but it needs to be said. All of that bullshit your family inflicted on you? It was awful and you were right to get yourself out of that toxic mess, but don't you think that your trauma scared you so that you are afraid to be vulnerable with *anyone* because that equates to losing all control over your own life? Letting someone else in doesn't mean shutting yourself out. There can be a happy medium there."

It was exactly the advice one of her characters would give another in her book. So why was it so hard to hear in real life? "How did you get to be so smart?"

"Honey," Karmel said with a world-weary chuckle. "I've kissed more than enough frogs in my life to know when there's a real prince in my immediate surroundings."

A prince with rough edges and sharp corners? Yeah, Nash had those. But he also had the heart of someone who wanted to help care for the people he loved so badly he couldn't stop himself from doing the wrong thing for the right reason. Logically, Chelle could see that. But in her heart, she was as scared as she'd ever been, and it made her entire body tense up. The instinct to cut herself off like she'd done with her family was so strong it made her palms sweaty. But Karmel was right.

Nash wasn't like the Finches.

"So, what do I do?" she asked, almost afraid to hear the answer.

Karmel finished her wine and stood up, lifting the thick strap of her airport tote over one shoulder. "Take the book deal."

"And Nash?" Chelle asked, her voice trembling.

"Honey, only you can figure that out." Karmel's phone vibrated in her hand. "My ride to the airport is here. Give me a hug and know I've got my fingers and toes crossed for you."

"Thank you," Chelle said as she wrapped her arms around her best friend and squeezed.

"Thank me by not ruining my record of one hundred percent of couples I've married still being together and madly in love," Karmel shot back as she strode out the door.

Yeah, if only Chelle knew how to do that. Instead, she was stuck here in her apartment where even the dogs were giving her the side-eye since Nash had left. From his favorite spot on the top of the bookcase to get stuck and yell angrily for help, Sir Hiss made pissed-off hissing noises.

"What, you can get up there but you can't get down?" She grumbled as she strode across the living room. "You know there's being stubborn and then there's just being obstinate. If you—"

The wisdom she was about to impart to the annoyed cat left her the moment she walked right into the corner of the coffee table, whacking her knee hard enough that she was pretty sure she could feel the pain in her right back molar. In that moment of absolute agony, everything came into focus. She looked at her living room—really looked at the placement of her furniture that she'd insisted Nash put back even though his arrangement had been better.

There was stubborn and there was obstinate, she'd been telling the cat. Maybe she should have been telling herself that—no, she definitely should have been talking to herself.

And in that millisecond, everything made sense, and she knew exactly what she needed to do and how she was going to make this right. All she had to do was make it through this afternoon's Christmas party and then she'd take the drive out to Gable House, brave the attack goose, and tell Nash—she had no fucking clue what she'd say, but she'd figure it out. She had to.

Of course, first, she needed to move some furniture.

Chapter Thirty-Two

Surrounded by mistletoe, garland, and potted poinsettias in her building's ornate meeting space that had once served as a glass-encased conservatory, Chelle had never wished more that she was anywhere else than the building Christmas party.

Okay, that was a lie. There was one specific place she wanted to be—with Nash. Too bad she'd fucked that up. Karmel was right. She may have—may have—okay, fine, had let her toxic baggage from her family take over and the results were shitty. All she knew was that she had to make it through the party and then she'd brainstorm what to say to Nash when she finally got next to him again.

So, she mixed and mingled and complimented everyone on their ugly Christmas sweaters, all the time watching the clock for a socially acceptable time to ditch the party, grab her dogs, and Uber her ass out to Gable House. It was on one of those furtive glances at the huge ornate clock that hung above the doors that she spotted the top of her uncle

Buckley's signature cowboy hat moving through the crowd.

She held onto her flute of champagne a little tighter, not wanting it to slip out of her suddenly clammy palms as her heart raced. Her uncle hadn't made an appearance at the foundation or her apartment since the judge's ruling came down. There was no way he was going to be anything but nasty when they came face-to-face. She did not have the energy for that today.

Downing the rest of her champagne, she scanned for the safest passage away from her uncle who, no doubt, was with the building's resident Grinch, Suzanne. Chelle's luck being Chelle's luck, however, meant that everywhere she turned there were people making any kind of getaway as slow as a slog through the snow with her short-legged dogs. She tried going toward the open bar but turned back almost immediately. Then she went left with the goal of getting through to the back exit that led to what had originally been the servants' stairs when the building had still been a Gilded Age mansion. She made it halfway there before two couples from the third floor started caroling so badly and off-key that everyone around them stopped dead to watch the train wreck.

Yeah. Maybe the open bar had not been one of her better decisions.

Determined to get out of there as her anxiety had her pulse roaring in her ears, she turned around—careful to avoid the cake table with the five-layer copy of the building iced with real buttercream—and nearly slammed into the crabbiest cowboy in the West himself.

Her gut dropped down to her toes.

"Well, if it isn't my favorite niece," Buckley said with a smarmy grin. "I see your lawyers got one past the judge."

Annoyance at his arrogance whipped her spine straight. "You mean they did their job and did a better job than your lawyers."

"For now." Buckley looked around dramatically, his gaze sliding over the people in the packed conservatory as if he'd just seen them for the first time. "Where's that so-called husband of yours?"

Beads of sweat dampened her hair at her temples as panic ate away at her ability to come up with a quick lie. There was no way she'd give Buckley the satisfaction of the truth, since she was determined to fix the mess she'd made of her marriage.

Finally, her brain clamped down a plausible fib that would hopefully lead to the least number of questions. "With his family."

Buckley tipped the brim of his cowboy hat back, revealing more of his sour face. "But not here supporting you during your big party?

"That's too bad." Suzanne hooked her arm through Buckley's and snuggled in close, nothing but schadenfreude gleaming in her eyes. "I'm sure it's breaking his heart not to be here with you."

"It's fine," Chelle ground out through clenched teeth.

These two were perfect for each other. Both of them mean-hearted control freaks who loved to exert whatever power they had. They were exactly like the evil wizard and his spell-spinner girlfriend in Chelle's books, who worked against her nymph assassins and satyr warriors for control of the forest and—

She let out a shocked gasp as everything fell into place at that moment, in her mind, so completely and instantly that she was surprised no one else in the room heard the pieces banging into place. The wizard in her books wore pointed-toe boots and what could be described as a very glittery cowboy hat. The spell spinner had the exact same short pixie haircut as Suzanne and even had the same mole at the base of her throat.

Why hello, subconscious, nice to see you're going strong even when I don't notice.

"Look at you keeping up a brave front," Buckley said in a loud voice with false cheer before lowering his volume and letting his natural bullying tone through. "Good luck trying to hold onto that energy when my lawyers get you on the stand. It'll make the whole procedure that much more enjoyable for me if you try."

All of the air whooshed out of her as fear grabbed hold of her with its sharp-taloned fingers. "But the judge already ruled that my marriage met the requirements of my dad's will."

Uncle Buckley took her ice-cold hand in his and patted the top of it patronizingly. "Poor girl. There is such a thing as appeals. Whether or not your marriage constitutes fraud is exactly the kind of thing I think the appeals panel will see my way." His lips curled upward into a grin that would have made her heart catch with worry if the anxious adrenaline wasn't already pumping it at twice its natural speed. "And wouldn't you just know that all three of the judges on the appeals panel are golfing buddies of mine? We meet up at the club every Tuesday."

The satisfied expression on his jerky little face said it all—fait accompli.

She pressed a fist to her stomach and tried to remember how to breathe, but the only thing filling her mind was the people who would be negatively impacted when Buckley shut down the foundation. It had all been for nothing. All the hard work of taking what had been a throwaway tax write-off and making it a force for good in Harbor City, her shithead of an uncle and the bullshit requirements of her dad's will, in the past.

She fucked it all up. All of it. The foundation. The books.

Nash. Everything.

That's when she heard the bark.

High pitched.

Happy.

Definitely yappy.

Turning, she spotted Nash walking over with both Mary Puppins and Groucho Barks in his arms. The dogs were ecstatically wagging their butts so hard they were practically levitating. Meanwhile Nash was glaring so hard at Uncle Buckley, Chelle wasn't sure he would notice if the dogs did start floating.

He stopped beside her, not behind her or in front of her acting like a human shield. While the dogs were distracted from her uncle by being right next to the humongous cake, Nash was not. When he did finally stop mean-mugging Buckley long enough to look down at her, everything about him loosened up. She felt the same shift in herself, like recognizing like, love recognizing love, home recognizing home.

"Hey, Chelle," he said, the double dimpler on full display.

Something warm and hopeful filled her chest until it seemed like there wasn't enough room in her lungs to take a breath. "Hi, Nash."

"Sorry I'm late." He lifted up his arms with the squiggly dogs. "I let myself into the apartment, but when I opened the door, these two sprinted out and made a beeline down the stairs, right for the party. I barely caught them before they ran into here."

"Those dogs are a menace," Suzanne snarled. "I promise you this, at the next tenant meeting I'm going to get the board to vote to make this place an animal-free building."

Uncle Buckley chuckled. "That sounds like a wonderful plan for these two fraudsters trying to make their so-called-temporary marriage seem like it was even the slightest bit real. I told you at your so-called wedding no one was going to believe someone like you would ever be enough for a man like him."

Mary and Groucho tensed, the fur along their spine going straight up, and started making the scariest sounding growl two pugs could do. Nash squared his jaw and his double dimples disappeared so fast it made Chelle's breath catch.

But instead of pushing his way forward or acting on his own, he turned to her and asked, his voice a harsh rumble, "Can I take care of these assholes for you?"

For a second, Chelle didn't know what to say. Here he was *asking* her, not assuming or mansplaining or any of the other bullshit. Yes, part of her wanted to yell "release the hounds" so the pugs could bite Suzanne's and Buckley's ankles bloody. Unfortunately, that wouldn't help things in the long run.

No, for that she needed to get devious. And she had just the plan.

"That. Is. It. I have had enough." She grabbed a flute of champagne from a passing waiter and chugged the whole thing as her uncle and Suzanne watched slack-jawed. When she shoved the empty glass into the top of the cake, it caused enough of a distraction that she had a second or two to not be the center of attention for everyone except Nash. He never took his eyes off of her.

She shot him a look that all but screamed "go with me on this" but couldn't say a word before everyone—and yeah, literally every pair of eyeballs in the room—was staring at her.

She glared at Nash. "I can't take it anymore. The constant advice no one ever asks for. The 'well actually' monologues. The diatribes that start with 'you know.' The verbal pats on the head because there's no way I could understand anything— even something as simple as how to walk my cat on a leash."

He flinched back, squinting at her in confusion. "Those

were all good ideas."

Fuck.

She thought he'd seen the look, would understand. She was debating shutting her entire plan down when he gave her a quick wink. Warmth washed through her, and she reached deep down for all the past resentments and frustrations from being pushed around by misogynistic assholes like her uncle.

"Oh yeah," she said, really leaning into the rush that came along with making a scene. "And moving my furniture just because you thought only you could pick the best place for my coffee table?"

The dogs wiggled in his arms, but Nash made holding them in place look easy. "But the cat—"

She interrupted without hesitation as the crowd stopped pretending to be doing anything but watching this trash fire. "Sir Hiss was fine with things the way they were before you barged into our lives and then repainted my kitchen!"

"If we're married—even temporarily—isn't it *our* kitchen?"

"Is your name on the deed?" She crossed her arms and drew herself up to her full height. "No, it's not, so it's my kitchen and you had no right to change my canary yellow paint. You don't get to control me!"

"Is there anything I am allowed to do?" Nash asked. "Or am I supposed to sit quietly in a corner rather than be ordered around like a puppy?"

"Oh, come on, we both know there were plenty of times when you wanted to be told exactly what to do," she scoffed.

A red flush ate its way up his face. "That's private."

"Is it?" She laughed even as on the inside she was praying that she hadn't taken the shitshow too far. "Is no one else allowed to have an opinion except for you? I've had more than enough of that. First with my dad, and then with this fake cowboy uncle of mine, and I have had it. I'm done with you. I'm done with all of you."

"You know, there really are better ways to express your frustrations," Nash said, talking to her as if she was a small child who, of course, was simply confused by the big, bad world. "For example, you could—"

"I can't take any of you and your mansplaining bullshit anymore." She let her head fall back and let out a loud, dramatic groan before straightening up and taking her dogs back from Nash. "I'm so glad we're getting a divorce."

There was a collective gasp in the room, but Chelle didn't stick around to watch the fallout from her little performance. All she could do was head back up to her apartment and hope like hell that Nash followed and she hadn't just ruined everything.

Chapter Thirty-Three

NASH

"I can give you the name of a great divorce attorney," Chelle's cowboy-cosplaying uncle said. "Just remember you dodged a bullet with that one. Guess I'll be calling the lawyers to stop the appeal. No one yells quite like a harpy except for a *real* wife. Trust me. I've had four."

It took everything Nash had not to squash the man like a cockroach. His hands were already fists at his side and he'd loosened his stance. What saved the dipshit, though, was the fact that Nash wanted to get back to Chelle more than he wanted to knock the other man into next week. It wasn't even close. He wanted to be with Chelle more than he wanted to breathe.

So instead of sending Buckley Finch sprawling with a right hook, Nash snarled at the older man, "Fuck straight off and stay the hell away from Chelle."

Then he headed toward the door, the crowd splitting in half as he strode to the stairs. He took them two at a time, his heart hammering against his chest, and sprinted down the hallway to Chelle's obnoxious and so very much her yellow front door. He hesitated with his hand on the doorknob. Did he walk right in? Did he knock? Had he fucked up what she was signaling?

He had no fucking clue what to do.

Then the door swung open and the pugs burst out, a cacophony of barks and a blur of fur. Nash barely noticed. All he could see was Chelle. She had on a hideous Christmas sweater with a goat eating all the presents under the tree knitted in red, white, and green, her dark hair was going a million different directions, and she was gnawing on her full bottom lip while nervously clasping and unclasping her hands.

She looked absolutely, 100 percent perfect.

"I wasn't sure you'd come," she said, a smile curling her lips.

Relief burned through him, melting the tension stringing him tighter than a watch turned too many times. He was moving before he realized it, closing the distance between them. "There was no way I could stay away any longer."

He cupped her face with both hands, desperate to kiss her, to pick her up and carry her to the bedroom, to do whatever it took to get her to take him back. But he shouldn't, not yet. He had to fix things first, make her understand that he'd never fuck up again. Okay, realistically, he'd mess up again because he wasn't perfect, but he'd fix it—just like he'd fix this.

"Chelle, I'm sorry." He had no idea what he was going to say, but the words still came out fast and honest from some deep place inside himself that he hadn't known was there— not until Chelle. "I fucked up because I was scared. Scared of losing you, scared of not being the one to make things easier for you, scared of who in the hell I was if I wasn't the one who took care of everything." His heart hammered against his ribs as panic and hope and a bone-deep plea to the universe had him on the edge of freaking the fuck out. "It's who I've been my whole life, and I have no clue who I am if not that, but I want to try to figure it out. And I want to do that with you, because I can't imagine doing that or anything else *without* you."

The tip of her nose turned bright red and she started blinking fast. "Nash, we need to talk." She stepped back so he could enter. "Please, come inside."

It felt like he was going to have a heart attack, or his brain was going to explode with the effort to keep his damn mouth shut, but he did. He followed her inside the apartment that felt like home because she was there.

He wasn't going to say *I love you* or push her in any way, not yet. No matter how much he wanted their future together to start now, he had to give her time. And he had every intention of staying true to that mission, but then she let out a shaky little sigh, a softer version of the sound she made when she came, and something inside him snapped.

Kissing her, he put every desperate hope, every foolish dream, and every sacred promise into it. There was more, so much more, but it would take a lifetime to show her every way she made him a better man. He tilted her head back, deepening the kiss as she let out little moans of pleasure that shot straight to his dick. Breaking the kiss was the last thing he wanted, but he had to do it.

"You were amazing down there," he said.

She pressed her fingertips to her kiss-swollen lips as she moved around him and closed her front door, leaning her back against it as the dogs disappeared into the living room. "I didn't mean any of it," she said, looking up at him as if she was afraid he'd missed her signal. "Not even one single part of it."

Unable to stop himself from touching her, he tucked a strand of hair behind her ear. "So the line about constant advice from me that you never ask for?" He pulled her closer so she was tucked against him, all of her curves fitting perfectly against him. "And moving your furniture?"

"Oh!" She pushed away from him. "I have to show you!"

She grabbed his hand and led him into the living room. It was as bright and quirky as the first day he'd stepped—well, hobbled—inside, but she'd moved all of the furniture. The bookcases were arranged so Sir Hiss could hop from the top of one to another. The couch had been scooted over to the wall where he'd put it on their wedding night. The oversize chair, though, was still in its original spot. He sat down in it, and instead of having her sit on the ottoman like she had when she'd examined his ankle, he pulled her onto his lap and wrapped his arms around her.

Chelle snuggled against his chest, laying her head on his shoulder. "I was going to tell you all about it when I got to Gable House. How I couldn't hear your advice because all I'd hear was the patriarchal bullshit of my family. I stuffed you in my emotional baggage, and that wasn't fair."

"I'm surprised I fit," he said, dipping his head lower so he could kiss his way down her neck.

She shivered against him and pivoted so she faced him, her hands going to the buttons on his shirt, slipping them free one at a time as he held his breath. Once they were all undone, she spread his shirt and trailed her fingertips down his chest, teasing him not only with her touch but also with the look on her face that said she wanted him as much as he wanted her.

"You are kinda big," she said before leaning down and brushing a kiss to the spot above his heart, "but I did practically carry you up my stairs that first day."

He started to laugh, but her busy hands went from his chest to the hem of her sweater, and he lost the ability to think when she lifted it over her head and tossed it to the ground. Part of him was yelling at him to stop her so they could have this conversation with their clothes on, but the rest of him pummeled that part to pieces. As long as he had eyes, he was going to want to watch Chelle Finch undress. The woman was fucking gorgeous, and he loved every part of her, from the silver streaks in her hair to the soft roundness of her belly to the thick thighs she'd used to help him get to her apartment that first day.

He'd spent his life helping other people, and she'd rescued him in every way possible from the moment they met.

"You were right about the layout," she said with a wry shake of her head. "Just like you were with the kitchen color."

"But not the book." Overstepping wasn't even a good enough word for what he'd done. He'd fucked up and had almost ruined everything. "That was wrong, and I'll happily spend the rest of my life making up for it. I should never have done that."

"No, you shouldn't have." She kissed him, a soft and sweet brush of her lips that still left him breathing hard. "But I'm going to say yes to the deal, and I'm going to dedicate the book to you. For the man with a huge heart and double dimples who changed my world and showed me that happily-ever-afters are possible in real life, too."

"Not to mansplain your feelings to you, but that sounds a lot like love," he said as he pulled her closer so she fit against his hardness, her velvety heat pressing against him.

God, this woman was going to kill him with pleasure, and he couldn't wait to spend the rest of his life with her, seeing if this was the time when being with her was so good it killed him.

"Well, actually, in this case you're right." She kissed him, her supple lips teasing and tempting him like only she could before she sat back. "I love you, Nash."

"I love you, Chelle."

And then he picked her up and carried her to the bedroom so he could show her exactly how much and in how many ways he loved her, and always would.

Chapter Thirty-Four

NASH

Christmas Morning...

The moment of truth had arrived.

Nash had woken up before the sun. Had there been a noise? Had Sir Hiss pounced on him in his sleep again? Who knew, but he was 100 percent awake without the aid of coffee or an alarm clock, watching the sky outside his old bedroom window at Gable House go from pitch black to soft pastels to the bright winter blue that promised snow later in the day. Tucked in against his chest, Chelle snored quietly. However, from their spot at the foot of the bed, Mary Puppins and Groucho Barks sawed logs loud enough to wake the dead.

Of course, those snores turned to ferocious barking when some dumbass pounded on the bedroom door.

"Get your ass up," Dixon hollered through the door. "It's time to open presents."

Nash had flung the comforter aside and was halfway

across the room while Chelle was still trying to blink herself awake—the woman needed a vat of coffee every morning just to function. He yanked open the door to find Fiona and Dixon standing in the hall. Fiona looked just slightly more awake than Chelle.

"I kept him in our room as long as humanly possible," Fiona said, her voice still rough from sleep. "I'm sorry."

Dixon didn't look sorry in the least little bit. Instead, he just smiled his shit-eating, I'm-gonna-win grin and let out a sharp whistle.

"Who wants breakfast?" he asked as he headed for the stairs, the pugs hot on his heels. "I can already smell the bacon Griff's making."

Fiona let out a tired sigh and shook her head before shuffling down the hall, tailed by Sir Hiss, who stayed a respectful stalking distance of three feet behind her.

"I'm gonna murder your cousin in a book," Chelle said as she got up from the bed, adjusting her sleep shorts and cropped tank top as she did.

"I'll buy a hundred copies," he promised.

Chelle chuckled and started to go through her morning series of stretches that gave Nash tantalizing glimpses of her thighs, stomach, and phenomenal tits when she moved.

"I guess we better get down there," she said as she rolled her head from side to side.

It took Nash a second to remember they had obligations outside of their bedroom, when all he wanted to do was toss Chelle back onto the bed and strip her down. That, however, he was going to have to wait for—his cousins would make sure of that.

"Yeah, he's definitely not going to stop being annoying until someone opens up Grandma Betty's present." He plucked the sprig of mistletoe up from the top of the dresser and walked over to Chelle, holding it over her head. "But first thing first."

He bent down and kissed her until they were both breathless. He really was going to have to kill Dixon for forcing them all to leave their rooms so early.

"Merry Christmas to me," she said, bringing her fingers to her kiss-swollen lips. "Now let's get down there. I can't wait to see you open your presents."

A plate of biscuits and gravy later (thank you, Kinsey's family recipe), Nash was sitting on the couch in the living room, holding a steaming mug of coffee strong enough that a spoon would stand straight up in it. Wrapping paper and colored tissue paper were littered on the floor and everyone had a small pile of gifts near where they sat. The dogs were asleep in front of the fireplace, Chelle was tucked up against his side with Sir Hiss asleep on her lap, and his numbnut cousins were arguing over how to pick who got to open Grandma Betty's present now that they'd all lost the Last Man Standing bet.

"Oh. My. God," Morgan said as she snagged two snickerdoodles from the tray of Christmas cookies on the coffee table. "Three-way rock, paper, scissors."

Dixon looked at Griff, who grunted his agreement and then shifted his gaze to Nash, who nodded.

They'd developed their version of the game over the summers they'd spent at Gable House as kids. The rules were simple. They each closed their eyes and tapped their closed fists on their palm three times. On the fourth tap, they opened their eyes and made either a closed fist for rock, a flat hand for paper, or two fingers outstretched for scissors. Paper beat rock. Rock beat scissors. Scissors beat paper.

One of each, they all lost, and therefore played another round.

One rock and two papers, the rock was out and the rocks played another round.

One rock and two scissors, both scissors were out. They went through as many lightning rounds of that until there was only one Beckett left.

Nash got up and stood with his cousins by the fireplace. Griff was out on the first round—never go paper first. The second round was a tie of double scissors. Dixon won the third round with a rock.

Everyone but Dixon and Fiona let out a groan.

Nash sat down on the couch next to Chelle, who gave him a sympathetic look.

"Sorry you lost," she said.

He shrugged, not caring in the least. "As long as I have you, I already have everything I could ever want," Nash said, brushing a kiss across her temple.

Cheesy? Abso-fucking-lutely. A hundred percent true? Without a single doubt.

Anyway, no matter what was inside the present, Nash knew that Grandma Betty had already outmaneuvered and outplayed him at his own game of manipulating people for their own good. He couldn't be happier about it.

Also extremely happy at the moment? Dixon, who was doing a victory lap around the living room.

Smug as ever, his cousin shot the room a self-satisfied grin and held out his hand for Grandma's present. "I'll take that, thank you very much."

• • •

DIXON

There was nothing in the world like a come-from-behind win—not even the best high in the world came close.

The only thing that rivaled sweet, sweet victory was any single thing that had to do with Fiona. Even the stuff that drove him nuts about her, like the fact that she was pretty much always right. For a man with an ego the size of the Northwest Territories (yeah, he was man enough to admit it), that hurt—almost as much as the fact that she kicked his ass every time they played Onze. He'd figure out a way to beat her. Eventually. They did have a whole lifetime together for him to find a way.

In the meantime, he had today's triumph to hold over his cousins' heads. Yeah, life was about as close to perfect at this moment as possible.

Morgan—who had taken possession of the present before any of the older cousins could snag it this morning—gave it to him. As everyone watched, Dixon made a big production of shaking the box next to his ear (it didn't make any noise) and holding it in his palm as if weighing it (mysteriously light). Then he lifted the rectangle wrapped in evergreen paper up to the light coming from the lamp by the oversize chair, where Fiona had folded herself up like a human pretzel. He squinted at the bottom of the package as if he could see through it.

Was he dragging this out?

Hell yes. He never said he wasn't an asshole.

"Dixon Beckett," Fiona said with a dramatic sigh. "I'm gonna tell everyone about your addiction to trashy reality TV if you don't put everyone out of their misery and open that present."

"You just told everyone," he said, clutching the gift to his chest in mock outrage like some Regency Era romance heroine she'd accused him of being when they first met.

"Not the names of the shows, like Ma—"

"Okay," he interrupted before she could spill the name of his favorite show—his cousins would never let him hear the end of it. "I'm opening it."

Everyone in the room started clapping and grumbling things like "finally" and "pain in the ass."

He sat down on the massive ottoman positioned at the

end of Fiona's chair. He sat the present down on his lap and smoothed his palms over the crinkly wrapping paper. Yes, he was still drawing this out—he was an asshole, remember—but he was also processing the fact that this really was the last gift from their grandmother that any of them would get. There was no way he could do this without taking at least a few seconds to say thank you to Grandma Betty.

The air shifted behind him as Fiona scooted forward, wrapping her arms and legs around him from behind before she laid her cheek against his back. She knew. Everyone in the room knew, which was why they'd stopped giving him shit and telling him to hurry up and open it already.

He slid his fingertips under one fold of the wrapping paper, unsticking the tape, and repeated the process until the paper fell away in his lap, revealing a plain white box. He lifted the lid, pushed the bright green tissue paper aside to reveal the mystery present, and started laughing.

• • •

GRIFF

Dixon's face was all soft and squishy and fucking smiley when he stopped doing the hyena giggle and looked down at the present. It was a look that in all their time growing up together, Griff had never seen on his cousin's face—especially not when he was about to bask in his winnings. Something was up.

"What is it?" Griff asked, craning to get a look at what was inside the open box.

Dixon shook his head and pulled out a knitted red, green, and white Christmas sweater that was roughly the size of his head. Stitched into the middle of it in green were the words "Great Grandma Loves Me." Then he turned the sweater around to reveal the words "Beckett Baby Number One."

Griff had already put the clues together before his cousin pulled out a second sweater identical to the first, except it said "Beckett Baby Number Two." Fiona reached into the box after that and picked up a third sweater with the words—yeah, no shocker—"Beckett Baby Number Three."

It took all of about three seconds for Griff to put the pieces together. He looked over at his fiancée, Kinsey, who was giving him the you-see-what's-happening look because, of course, she worked the whole thing out half a second before he had. They had a quick silence go between discussion about it, and then he grunted his agreement with her assessment. Grandma Betty definitely wasn't done with the oldest Beckett cousins quite yet.

"You know what this means, right?" Dixon asked as his focus ping-ponged between Griff and Nash.

"Another bet," Griff said as he shook his head, because there was no use fighting the inevitable.

Yes, they were competitive jerks, but it's who they were, and Grandma Betty had known how to use that to her advantage—turned out the Last Man Standing bet had been to their advantage, too, now that each of them had gone from confirmed bachelor to happily in love in the past year.

Nash picked up one of the sweaters and held it up as if he was judging the size. "A race to produce the next generation of Becketts?"

Kinsey, Fiona, and Chelle all rolled their eyes. Griff couldn't blame them any more than he could turn down the bet that was about to be agreed to.

Cocky as ever, Dixon shot his cousins a shit-eating grin. "Oh, the sacrifices I have to make just to beat you two again."

"So you're both agreed?" Nash held out his hand. "Babies win?"

Griff and Dixon nodded and took turns shaking his hand. It wasn't until Nash started laughing that Griff realized where he'd gone wrong.

"Asshole," he grumbled at Nash.

• • •

NASH

Victory wasn't just sweet. It was fucking perfect.

"I believe those are mine." He held out his hand. "I did adopt them, after all."

Chelle smothered a laugh before adding, "He insisted the lawyer draw up the papers before the holiday."

Dixon looked over at him in confusion for half a second before his smart-ass grin faded and the realization hit. He looked over at Griff as if searching for an ally, but their cousin just shrugged and grunted. Translation: Nash Beckett had won. While Fiona giggled and Kinsey lifted her teacup in toast, Dixon rolled his eyes and handed over Grandma Betty's gift.

Nash lifted the three red, white, and green sweaters over his head in triumph. "To the fur baby winners—Sir Hiss Finch-Beckett, Mary Puppins Finch-Beckett, and Groucho Barks Finch-Beckett."

The animals had no clue what all the fuss was about, but the pugs still yapped as they accepted snickerdoodle crumb bribes while he pulled the sweaters over their heads, and the cat just stayed laying on its side on the floor, meowing pitifully about the humiliation of having to wear a sweater when his turn arrived.

"You're loving this, aren't you?" Chelle asked as she took pictures of him holding up the very unenthusiastic Sir Hiss.

"Absolutely," he said before putting the cat down and joining his fiancée on the couch. "Somewhere up there, Grandma Betty has to be smiling, because her brilliant ploy had worked exactly as she'd planned."

It was true—even for him. And he couldn't be happier. He had the woman he loved, the fur babies he adored, and a life that he hadn't imagined possible. Plus, now he'd won the latest competition. Did it get better than that? He didn't think so.

Chelle snuggled into his side as they watched the rest of the Becketts and soon-to-be-Becketts laugh and take pictures of the animals in their new sweaters. "Do you think the younger cousins think they're free and clear?"

"Yeah," Nash said. "But they're wrong."

"What makes you say that?" she asked, looking up at him.

"Because no one loved happily-ever-afters more than Grandma Betty." He dipped his head down, stopping just short of kissing his now and forever wife. "I know she gave us ours. I love you, Mrs. Chelle Finch-Beckett."

"I love you, too," she said before meeting him halfway in a kiss that made the whole rest of the world disappear.

Acknowledgments

I know all of the readers have been waiting (sorta) patiently on this one. Thank you so much for caring about the Beckett cousins and trying to figure out what that final present from Grandma Betty would be. I hope Nash's story hit all the high notes for you. A huge thank you to Liz, Lydia, Jessica M. and the entire Entangled team for sticking with what was beginning to feel like a cursed book. I'd share my Oreos with y'all any day. As always, I couldn't do this without my family. Thank you!!!

About the Author

USA Today and *Wall Street Journal* bestselling romance author Avery Flynn has three slightly wild children, loves a hockey-addicted husband, and is desperately hoping someone invents the coffee IV drip. She lives with her family (including the dogs Gravy, Pepper, Tater Tot, and Eggnog, who are either sleeping or guarding the house from squirrels as well as the cat, Dwight, who is totally plotting world domination) outside of Washington, D.C. She loves to chat with readers. You can email her at avery@averyflynn.com and join her reader group, The Flynnbots, on Facebook!

averyflynn.com

Discover more romance from Entangled...

KISSING GAMES
a Kissing Creek novel by Stefanie London

Pro baseball player Ryan Bower is back in his small hometown, recovering from an injury. All he wants is a little rest and relaxation. But librarian Sloane Rickman has turned his world upside down, with her erotic book club picks and quirky sense of humor. Ryan can't afford to get tangled up with someone rooted in Kissing Creek—his career takes him everywhere but. And these kissing games they're playing could end up being lose-lose...

THE BEST KEPT SECRET
a Where There's Smoke novel by Tawna Fenske

When nurse Nyla Franklin's best friend spills his biggest secret ever, Nyla knows she's not just holding a secret. She's holding a ticking time bomb. Mr. Always Does the Right Thing Leo Sayre's post-surgery confession has everything flipped upside down and turned inside out...including his relationship with Nyla. Secrets have a way of piling up, and it's just a matter of time before someone lights a match. Because while the truth can set you free, it can also burn completely out of control...

Made in the USA
Monee, IL
06 April 2025

15190801R00144